BODY IN THE CATHEDRAL

A RITA PATEL MYSTERY

By Catherine Cooper

Oxford eBooks

Chapter

1

Friday 27th December 2019 4pm

Rita Patel froze. The shot was close to her right ear. The reverberating sound as the bullet hit the cupboard nearly knocked her off balance. She could not risk giving away her hiding place by falling and making a noise. With a gunman waiting that could be fatal.

The cupboard was quite an old one and, apart from Rita, it was empty. It was tall and wide, so at five feet seven she could just about stand up in it. Her refuge had probably been used for coats in the past, she guessed. It had looked quite old when she had jumped through its door. It reminded her of the wardrobe in the Narnia books she had read as a child, but, unfortunately for her, it was not the portal to another world. It was solidly built, however, as things from the past often were, she had found, and, most importantly, it was made of steel. The bullet must have bounced off the side.

Rita started to recover from the shock and to appraise her situation. Her phone was on silent and probably wouldn't get a signal inside this tin can anyway. Her clothes were dark and practical. Before she had left her flat, she had tucked a black crew neck jumper into skinny jeans, and on her feet she had her black ASOS trainers. Over this she wore the black padded jacket she had bought just before Christmas, from Primark in the Haymarket shopping centre of her home town, Leicester.

It was late afternoon when she had gone into the building and dived into the cupboard, which was inside the front entrance. She had acted on impulse. Now she was regretting it. She would be okay if she could stay undiscovered until it was dark and then escape, Rita reasoned to herself. She could afford to wait. She had said she was going into town to look at some war memorials. She would not be missed for a few hours.

With luck, whoever was in the building would leave at some point and she could work out how to get away, she told herself, trying to lift her spirits. Her beany hat had fallen from her head in her dash inside what she had taken to be a refuge. Her long, brown, curly, hair was springing out in all directions in its usual fashion. There was no point in worrying about it, Rita thought, as she listened intently for any more noises coming from outside the cupboard. How had she got into this fix?

The weather over the Christmas break had been relatively mild. It had rained the previous day, which was Boxing Day, but today, Friday, it had been dry. Rita had been in the town centre when she caught sight of the man by chance. The town was relatively quiet. All the bustle of the Christmas Fairs had been removed. The main reminder this was a festival period were the lights which were strung across the roads around Town Hall Square. They had been there since the start of Diwali in November and were showing signs of fatigue.

She had been standing on Every Street, near the Town Hall, indulging in her latest hobby. She was examining the memorial to the fallen in the Boer war. It was a substantial three-sided affair made of stone and bronze with rows of names of those who had died in the conflict, which took place in South Africa between 1899 and 1902. In the middle and on the two sides of the memorial were elaborate statues of what looked like angels distressed by grief. It was in a quiet spot close to a busy square, and all the more moving for that. Why do we never learn the lessons? she had been thinking when she looked up and saw a face she recognised. The face of a person she knew, but did not trust.

On impulse she had followed him on foot, thinking to herself that this was becoming a habit. She tried to keep the man in her sight, but stay back to prevent him from realising she was there. Thinking about it now, as she tried to breathe quietly in the cupboard, Rita thought they had probably walked for about twenty minutes, maybe more. Her quarry had led her right onto nearby Horsefair Street, left into the road that led to the market and then right towards the main shopping street of Gallowtree Gate, where keen shoppers were seeking bargains in the sales. Rita had thought she might lose him among the people strolling in the pedestrianised area, and she wondered if her prey was intending to make some purchases. He did not pause to take up any of the retail opportunities on offer, however. Instead, at the point where Gallowtree Gate intersects with Church Gate, the man had paused and stood for a moment talking into his phone. He was scanning the horizon while he did this, so Rita had ducked into a shop doorway and changed her hat. This was a trick she had learnt from a private detective she had met in Italy; Rita kept a couple of hats in her bag for just such an occasion. She tried to stay unnoticed. Her quarry by contrast was wearing a yellow padded jacket which made him easy to spot from a distance.

The pair walked on, turning into St Margaret's Way, where the road was busy with traffic. Those who had been cooped up with their families over the break were seeking solace in retail therapy, it seemed, even at the cost of queuing for car parks. There were fewer pedestrians here to camouflage Rita. They had just reached the part of the road which crosses over the river, when the man turned right and Rita could see they were headed for Abbey Park.

Rita knew the park well. Although the eponymous abbey had been in ruins since the Reformation of the Church in the 16th century, as a keen student of history Rita knew it was at the abbey that Cardinal Wolsey had died after he fell out with King Henry VIII. There was a memorial to him in the grounds. It seemed to be a day for memorials, she thought to herself as she waited to see where the man was leading her. He was walking with confident steps. Where was he going? He led her along the river which divided the park in two, past the lake, where Rita had once almost drowned, and then out through tall wrought iron gates. Now they were in a rundown street lined with buildings which in their heyday had been thriving hosiery and textile factories and warehouses.

It was towards one of these buildings that the man crossed the road purposefully. He clearly knew where he was going. Rita had watched from a distance as he paused in the middle of the street to talk to a boy on a bike. Just as he did so, Rita's phone vibrated in her pocket. She glanced down at the screen. It was a call from her younger brother, Nayan.

Rita lifted the phone to her ear. "Not now!" she hissed.

At the old factory which was her quarry's destination the wooden front door, which had green paint flaking off it, had opened automatically as he approached. He marched straight in, leaving the door behind him ajar. Her phone still in her hand, Rita had swiftly followed. It had seemed a good idea at the time.

As soon as she had got inside the disused factory, she could hear voices. It was then she had taken the fateful decision to play for time and hide in the cupboard in the hallway. It was only a short while later that the gun had been fired. So, the occupants must know she was there. How was that? It seemed unlikely that the man knew she was following him, or her subject would not have been so casual, Rita reasoned. Perhaps there was a camera on the door, even though the building looked too old to have that kind of security? Whatever had caused her presence to be discovered, it was not turning out very well, she had to concede.

Friday 27th December 2019 4.00 pm

The young boy on a bike, circling one-handed, a mobile phone in his other hand, was a bit of a cliché, Detective Chief Inspector Jamie Bridge felt, watching the lad with the benefit of the cameras which the police force had hidden on buildings adjoining the site under surveillance. The DCI was two streets away, in an office which was one of several made out of a renovated Victorian warehouse. Leicestershire police had taken over a floor in the office building temporarily, such was the perceived importance of this operation. They had two rooms and a kitchen at their disposal.

The other two floors, one above and one below, were rented by solicitors and accountants. They were small firms dealing with the lower end of society and their problems. The businesses advised on a daily diet of benefit appeals, immigration cases and disputes with the Inland Revenue, and their clientele entered and left the building at all hours of the day and well into the evening. Any police officers in plain clothes discreetly coming and going through the main entrance would be taken as clients. During the night hours officers, dressed as security guards, used the rear entrance where, conveniently, there was a small car park.

A team had been allocated to the surveillance, with the officers involved replacing each other every four hours to keep them fresh. It was easy for boredom to settle in, and then details would be missed. Having to be conducted over the Christmas period, it was proving a costly operation and the overtime claims were through the roof. The room in which DCI Bridge was sitting, his head resting on his chin thoughtfully, contained three screens on which they could monitor the disused hosiery factory. This was, according to their informants, the centre of a major drug manufacture and distribution operation, right in the heart of the city of Leicester. The factory, near Abbey Park Road, had recently been acquired by developers and was poised to be levelled to the ground to make way for a five-storey apartment block which, it was said in the planning application, would 'provide a new beneficial building with architectural merit'. The imminent demolition had led to the urgency of the police operation. No one knew when the criminals would pack up and ship out to a new location, and, if the police did not act now, all the intelligence they had managed to gather would be wasted.

There was tension in the team, stemming from major cuts to the force combined with pressure from above to improve the success rate in the fight against crime. A lot of resources from their limited budget had gone into the surveillance. From what they had seen, and through phone messages that had been intercepted, between two major players, who called themselves 'Chewbacca' and 'Han Solo', it had looked like the main instigators would be meeting at the factory that day. So much official effort and planning had gone into today that they needed arrests, they needed results. Basically, they needed crime to be committed before their eyes.

A lot of criminal activity, like lawful businesses, was run online these days, Jamie Bridge was thinking to himself as he waited for the second suspect to enter the building. It meant it was rare to encounter the perpetrators in person, let alone to have the chance to arrest some of the 'management'. They would never catch the people at the very top of the organisation. They could only be seen in glossy magazines which depicted the urban rich at play in Monaco or San Tropez or on their own Caribbean island. The twists and turns of the trail would ensure there was no way of tracing the crimes back to them.

From intelligence gathered in other operations, he knew the proceeds of the drug operation would be taken abroad in cash, converted to jewellery or other high value items which would then be sold in places like Dubai. The resulting funds would then be moved through a spin cycle of offshore companies in tax havens round the world. Some of it found its way back into the UK and bought up property in fashionable places like Notting Hill and Hampstead in London. Jamie Bridge had once been driven along Bishops Avenue, one of the wealthiest streets in the world, by a DCI from the Met. The houses there sold for millions. Even a four-bed flat was on the market for nearly £7 million, he had discovered from an online property site. It was hard to see how ordinary people could afford them. House after palatial house had looked empty. The street was like a ghost town. "Sometimes the help live in the basement" the Metropolitan Police officer had told him, "Like Downton Abbey, isn't it?" he remarked, "They have regular security patrols by a private firm to protect their investment. But nobody actually lives there."

It was unlikely the force would lift any of the crime proceeds today, but at least the operation would disrupt the organisation and supply chain for a bit, DCI Bridge thought, as he stood to yawn and stretch his back, still looking at the monitors. Temporary inconvenience was all they could hope for. It felt like they were fighting a losing battle. The criminals had better intelligence, were better equipped and resourced than the police, who still operated in 43 different forces across England, each liaising with some national groups like the Crime Agency. The only thing the criminals lacked was loyalty. They bought allegiance through fear and intimidation. It meant there was always someone, like their informers, prepared to risk the retaliation of their colleagues in exchange for a lighter sentence or witness protection, if the powers that be would agree to it. To his regret, it was looking like their informers, who had not been protected, had paid the ultimate price for their treachery. DCI Bridge had been forced by the surveillance op to hand over that part of the investigation to Inspector Lu, another overworked senior officer. For continuity, Lu was working with two of Jamie's team, when they could spare the time of course.

The figure they had been waiting for crossed into his vision at last. The DCI saw him stop and exchange something with the boy on the bike. It was probably a new pay- as -you-go phone, the Detective Chief Inspector surmised. That was a shame, but predictable. It cut off the police from a useful source of information. The boy rode off the edge of the monitor. The person they were interested in went into the factory building. The phone in DCI Bridge's pocket vibrated. It was Sue Foster, the Assistant Chief Constable, who was in command of this operation.

"Chewbacca and Han Solo are both in there?" she asked cryptically.

"Yes Ma'am" he said.

"Time to move in." she ordered from her office in Enderby.

Looking round the makeshift furniture in the surveillance room, Jamie Bridge recalled the dark blue leather corner sofa in his ACC's office, which matched the Indian blue patterned curtains from John Lewis which she had had installed at the windows. Office gossip had it they cost £140 a pair. Sue Foster was probably also sipping a decent cappuccino, not making her way through yet another cup of instant coffee which Jamie Bridge had made for himself using the kettle in the kitchen/diner shared by the surveillance officers.

"Trissey! Yousef!" the DCI called to the members of his team who were in the kitchen/diner at that moment enjoying biscuits and a hot drink. As the young detective constables came through to join the DCI, all three trained their eyes on the monitors. Soon they would be inside that building and speaking to the two men they had only witnessed silently so far. It had been judged too risky to try to get equipment into the factory so they could listen in. The nearest microphone was on one of the adjoining buildings.

"What the…?" DCI Jamie Bridge stopped half way through pulling on his jacket to stare open mouthed at the screen.

"Who is that?" DC Trissey Adams asked, moving closer to one of the screens to get a better look.

"We aint seen her before, boss." DC Yousef Mohamed said with concern, his brow furrowing.

"What is she doing there?" the pitch of the DCI's voice rose as he spoke, and he clenched his teeth as he watched.

A female was indeed entering the factory under surveillance. She was Asian in appearance, mid-twenties in age, and about five foot seven inches in height. The figure which the three officers were watching was wearing black trousers, and jacket, and had curly brown hair protruding from a turquoise beany hat.

"Rita Patel!" the DCI gasped. She was going to ruin the operation, he thought despairingly.

* * *

"Abort! Abort!" DCI Jamie Bridge was shouting into the radio that connected him to other officers, who were poised to enter the factory and arrest those present. It was too risky to do so with a civilian on the premises, although who knew why Rita was there.

He had only just issued the order, when the one microphone they had managed to install near the factory picked up a sound. It was a sound which the three officers recognised immediately. The gunshot issuing from the building caused them all to freeze for a moment. Jamie Bridge's phone vibrated with a message. He glanced down at it.

It was from Rita's brother, Nayan "WTF?! Rita was talking to me on her phone, then I heard a gunshot! Tell me she's OK?"

"I'm on it. Hang tough." he messaged back quickly before barking instructions to the Detective Constables in the room to call up armed response and a negotiating team, while he took another call from the Assistant Chief Constable, Sue Foster.

"I hear shots have been fired." she began.

"A shot, yes." he confirmed.

"There's a civilian in the building?" she asked. Jamie Bridge realised his boss had been watching the feed from the factory on her monitor.

"Yes Ma'm." he confirmed, thinking it wise to keep to himself the identity of the civilian, at least until they knew more about what was going on. "Armed response is on its way." he told the Assistant Chief Constable.

"Use your discretion 'til they get there." she said, unhelpfully. "I'm coming down there myself. I'll assume Gold Command."

Oh great, thought Jamie Bridge, so if anything goes wrong it's my fault and, if it all goes well, you'll take the credit. It was no mystery to him how Sue Foster had risen up the ranks so quickly while he had been stuck at DCI for a few years now.

"Surround the building." he ordered, "But keep out of range of any gun."

The three of them left the operations room, clattered down the metal fire escape that led outside from the kitchen/diner and into the car park at the back, alarming the other occupants of the offices and blowing their cover. They jumped into a black Ford Mondeo and raced towards the disused factory, Yousef pinning the flashing blue light to the roof of the car as Trissey drove and the DCI issued instructions to the rest of the team.

Who had fired a gun? What kind of gun was it? They had not seen any firearms going in, and their informants had not mentioned weapons. Was anyone hurt? These and other questions were rushing through Jamie Bridge's mind, like a series of racing cars on a formula one track. Above all, why had this happened just after Rita Patel entered the building? And was Rita all right?

Chapter

2

"History and beauty lie in the baroque wrinkles of old cathedrals, mosques, synagogues, temples and faces whose stories are told without a single word."

Khan Kijarro Nguyen

Friday 27th December 2019 4.10 pm

Through the cupboard door, Rita Patel could hear the wail of emergency vehicle sirens, starting in the distance but getting nearer, which suggested to her she might need to change her plan. She was in real trouble now, she thought.

"Don't shoot! It's Rita!"

In the darkness, Rita heard her name being spoken by the man she had been following.

"Rita?" another man, presumably the one with the gun, said, "Rita…Rita who?" He sounded breathless and confused.

The first man spoke again, "Come out, Rita, he won't shoot you!"

Rita started to open the cupboard door from the inside; she moved cautiously, not sure what she could do if the gun was fired again. Just as she was adjusting her backpack onto her right shoulder to attempt an exit with a degree of elegance, someone quickly pulled the door wide open and she stumbled out. Rita staggered as she tried to regain her balance, and found herself with a gun in her face. It was a small weapon, like the kind gangsters tuck into their belts in movies. Looking up from the gun, she had a shock. She recognised the holder only too well. Except that he was the last person that Guy Ritchie would cast in one of his films, she thought.

"It's you!" Rita and the gunman said at the same time. They recognised each other from their place of work. How was it possible that the person she had been following, and the man who was now confronting her with a gun, knew each other? And why was the gunman here at all? Rita's mind went into overdrive. Colin Shawcross was the last person she had expected to see, Rita thought, a vivid picture of one of their encounters flashing into her mind.

Tuesday 10th September 2019 10.00 am

"Grab your note book. See you outside in five!" By September, Rita had been an intern at the law firm for a couple of months. Edward Maitland, the father of her friend Morwenna, had arranged it. She had started in the summer in the Probate Department, where she had enjoyed the work related to clients' wills and estates, but, just as she was getting the hang of it and feeling she could make a contribution, she had been moved to criminal work, where she felt like a fish out of water. Still, she had to admit it was important for her to sample all parts of the firm with a view to progressing towards a training contract. Not only would this bring payment for her labours, but, together with passing the Legal Practice Course, it would enable her to qualify as a solicitor. First, though, she had to survive the Criminal Department.

Rita had learned several things since moving to the basement, where the criminal work of the practice was carried out. The location prevented, on the whole, any mixing of the criminal clients, as it were, with the commercial and private clients. There was little natural light down there, so it was a good idea to get in early and grab a work station near the glass door by the fire escape. The lawyers in the Criminal Department only drank coffee at their workstations and saw this as matter of pride. "The Property Department drink tea."

they told her. Rita had therefore brought in her own mint tea bags, which she kept in her locker together with her mug and laptop, when not in use. The hours were erratic, because crime was not committed between nine and five, and there was a lot of waiting around, whether it was at the court, the prison, or the police station.

Rita had also learned that a surprising number of people go missing in the system. Even on her first day in the Criminal Department, the prison authorities and private contractors had contrived to transport the wrong prisoner to a hearing, wasting who knows how much time and money. All the agencies blamed each other, of course. In the end their client had appeared late in the day via a rather temperamental video link. There were stories all the time in the office about the wrong people being released and others who, when they had tried to visit, had been moved to another prison, but no one could say where.

Rita had been told by her fellow interns to expect Colin Shawcross, one of the senior lawyers, to be difficult to work with. The Department was short-handed and after a couple of days of witnessing how Colin Shawcross behaved Rita was beginning to see why. His communication to her was, as usual, pre-emptory. Sighing, she rose from her chair and switched off the laptop in front of her, lifting it to stow it away with her other possessions. Any notes she needed to take could be done on her iPad which she put in her backpack. She regretted having to move. It was doubtful she would see that same chair again that day, and she had liked its position. The other interns kept their heads down as Rita passed them across the open plan office. They were either eyeing up Rita's spot, and preparing to make their move for it, or thanking their lucky stars that it was Rita who Colin Shawcross had picked on and not them.

Having climbed the staircase to the lavish lobby area of the firm, where the receptionists sat among large potted plants with fixed smiles on their faces, like cabin crew on a plane, Rita stumbled through the automatic doors into the natural light on the pavement outside on Belvoir Street, in the centre of Leicester. Rita had her black backpack perched on her right shoulder and her raincoat clutched in her left hand. September had so far proved to be a month of sun and sudden showers. Mr Shawcross (as he liked to be addressed, much to the secret amusement of the rest of the office) had not said where they were going, but it was a fair bet it would be a police station or a prison. He had been in the Criminal Department of the firm for a few years, but was still an associate and not a partner. He had a busy criminal practice. "I know all the local villains" he never tired of telling young, aspiring lawyers.

"Eventually they go down for something, but not necessarily the crime they themselves committed." he had told Rita on their first taxi journey to Leicester prison. It was swings and roundabouts he told her, a bit like the VAR system they were bringing into football. Sometimes the system went with you and sometimes it didn't.

It was the destination of Welford Road Prison that Colin Shawcross barked at the driver through the front passenger window of the taxi as soon as it stopped. The men's prison was in the centre of town, north of Nelson Mandela Park. Opened in 1828, its appearance resembled a medieval castle and was often mistaken for such by visitors. The gatehouse and part of the walls were regarded as architecturally important and were Grade 2 listed, Rita knew. During the era of capital punishment twenty-three people had been executed there after its opening in 1953, Rita had read, and well-known inmates had included Charles Bronson and the Kray twins.

Rita had been trying to put on her mac as another sharp shower started to teem from the skies. The solicitor opened the back door of the vehicle and climbed in, leaving Rita to dive in after him and shut the door just as the taxi pulled away from the kerb. She had not had time to do up the buttons on her coat and her hair was slipping free from its scrunchie. There was no point worrying about her appearance, given the destination, she thought. Colin Shawcross was not bothered; he barely registered Rita's presence and only wanted her with him to take notes and do any donkey work arising. That was something else she had learnt about how a criminal practice is conducted. The legal aid rates that the firm received were parsimonious, so the only way to make the work pay at all was to allocate tasks to the cheapest members of staff, and you did not get any cheaper than Rita, and the other unpaid interns.

It was probably the lack of lucrative fees that had hindered Colin Shawcross in his progress in the firm, Rita thought, looking across at him. That and his dress sense, or lack of it. She was travelling backwards on the pull-down seat of the black cab, the sort you saw all over the streets of London. Rita was glad to have chosen trousers to wear with her jacket that day. It was hard to make your legs look elegant while perched on that seat. Colin Shawcross was sprawled across the back seat opposite her, not worrying about elegance. His large brown battered briefcase and shabby raincoat were occupying the seat next to him. He was probably in his late thirties, or early forties, Rita considered, with a hairline which was receding at the front while untidy wisps of mousy brown hair at the sides flopped forward when he lowered his head over his papers. His suit was not fashionable – the male interns called him 'M&S man'- and his shoes were scuffed at the toes.

Despite his appearance, however, the lawyer's boasts of a successful practice seemed to be true, from what Rita had seen so far. He had a good reputation among the criminal fraternity, if that was a thing, she thought. People who had been through the system would ask for him again and he was virtually on a retainer for some of the local criminal families, who had members in and out of prison on a frequent basis. They were the ones who were unlucky enough to be caught. With police forces stretched owing to reductions in the number of officers, it was reported that only about 14% of crimes were actually being detected to the point of prosecution and that the public, losing faith in the police, were often not reporting crimes like theft. So, the Criminal Department was only seeing the tip of the iceberg, Rita concluded.

"Not staying, I hope" the Asian driver, a middle-aged man with a bald head and a large paunch squeezed under the steering wheel, joked about their destination as if they had never heard anyone say that before.

"Hopefully not" Colin Shawcross gamely responded and even managed a cross between a smile and a grimace, revealing his crooked and somewhat yellowing teeth, as he took off his reading glasses and put some papers back in his briefcase before checking his phone and finally looking at Rita.

"Prisoner on remand." he explained, exuding coffee breath in her direction, "Wants to change his representation. Charge is GBH with intent."

"Pretty serious then." Rita put in. The few assault cases she had come across so far were the result of fights, often after too much alcohol or as part of a road rage incident. Drinking and driving were clearly both bad for your health. A charge of GBH with intent suggested something more one-sided, or premediated, she thought.

The interview with the prisoner that followed started to run like a video in Rita's head as she waited to see what other shocks Colin Shawcross, gun in hand, had for her. Had there been something 'off' about that meeting with the prisoner? Rita had been too new at the time to have much to compare it with, but over the weeks since, and building up her experience with other senior members of the firm, she had come to realise that Colin's approach was less than conventional, to say the least. Indeed, although he got good results for his clients, it was often hard to see how these were achieved.

Tuesday 10th September 2019 10.30 am

Leeroy Roberts had slouched rather than walked into the interview room in the prison. He sat at the table opposite Rita and Colin, and promptly laid his head down on the table.

"Come on now!" the warder who had accompanied Leeroy, and was standing in the corner of the interview room, chided him. "This is your brief. Your chance to sort out your case."

Colin smiled. "We'll be OK, won't we Leeroy?" he said, "No need for you to stay, officer, we'll buzz when we've finished."

Leeroy sat up at this and nodded his agreement to this arrangement.

"Well, all right." the warder said and left the room.

Rita sat apprehensively, waiting for what might happen. Did Colin know what he was doing? Was it safe to be left with an offender - sorry, suspect - accused of a serious assault?

"We haven't got much time." Colin began. He wrote something on a legal notepad. "That's the figure." he said. Leeroy looked at it and grunted.

Colin took the pad back and screwed up the piece of paper.

"So, we get the charge reduced..." Colin began.

"I weren't there" Leeroy protested.

Colin sighed, "Look, you know how this works. You weren't there, but where you were would get you in a whole load of other trouble, so let's just keep this simple shall we?

Bail and a suspended sentence, that's what we're aiming for."

Rita wasn't sure about the word simple. She had thought they would be going through the evidence, sorting out the grounds of Leeroy's defence, but Colin had written Leeroy a note she hadn't seen and had then gone on to discuss the charge and the sentence. He was also suggesting he could get the suspect out on bail. Would the court agree to that? she wondered.

"Rita," Colin turned to her, "Make a note that we agreed to contact the CPS about the charge and get Leeroy before the court to argue for bail."

Rita wrote, as directed, on her iPad.

"I'll make the call now." Colin said, "She'll be OK with you, won't she?" he addressed the prisoner, referring to Rita.

"Sure boss" Leeroy replied.

Rita tried to hide her concern. Where was that buzzer the guard had mentioned?

* * *

"You've no idea what it's like in here." With Colin out of the room, Leeroy was suddenly alert and in full flow. "I can't wait to get on the other side."

"I gather it's a bit overcrowded here." said Rita, who had read the figures. More than 18,000 prisoners across the estate were cooped up in overcrowded cells and three out of five men's prisons were holding more people than they were certified to look after. This led to high levels of violence and hindered rehabilitation. Several prisons had been placed in special measures, although Leicester Welford Road was not one of them. England and Wales had the largest prison population in Western Europe. We seem to like locking people up, Rita had thought. In total about 79,700 men and 3,800 women were imprisoned in the previous year, representing 0.084% of the population. Every so often, there would be moves to release some prisoners early, which had its own disadvantages, especially if the Parole Board was not properly consulted, and, in any event, as fast as groups were released, the judges sentenced others to detention. The system was crying out for reform, but, like all public services, had been starved of resources for several years.

"Overcrowding doesn't begin to cover it. There isn't room to swing a cat! You can't get away from the other prisoners. Even in your cell, anyone can come in at any time, and basically do anything to you, you know what I mean?" Leeroy was a big powerful-looking young man, but his eyes were glistening as he sought understanding from Rita.

"But what about the staff, the prison guards?" she asked.

"That's a joke, innit?" Leeroy scoffed. "You saw how quickly Dave - that's his name - scarpered when Colin suggested it. They're outnumbered. Sometimes there might be as many as six screws to a hundred prisoners, sometimes less. You could go all day without seeing one."

Rita shook her head in disbelief.

"Who keeps order then?" she asked.

"Hah!" he replied derisorily, shaking his head of thick black hair and sitting back in his chair, enjoying having an audience for once. "The gangs. They run the prisons now. You've no choice. Join them or get crushed by them. There are two main gangs here, and they keep us on separate landings as far as they can, to reduce the violence. The gangs are in charge, though"

"How can they do that?" Rita wanted to know.

"They control everything, mainly through the drugs. You can get drugs more easily inside prison than on the outside, if you've got the money or will work for it that is. Most prisons run on Spice. Often new prisoners are given it without them knowing, in a free cigarette. They lose all inhibitions. It's entertainment for the other prisoners. And, once they're hooked, they'll do whatever the gangs want so they can get another fix, moving on to cannabis and then heroin. It's all available on tap."

"How does it get in here?" Rita wanted to know, aghast at the lawlessness taking place behind closed doors.

"The gangs again. They have ways of smuggling the drugs in. And some of the screws are bent as well. They help. But I've said too much." he stopped abruptly as Colin came back.

"All sorted." he said, "The CPS will reduce the charge and we'll have a bail hearing on Friday. Don't worry about it." Colin sounded very confident, Rita thought. "Get the business done before then. We'll talk about the other matter when you're bailed?"

"Fine by me boss" Leeroy assented.

Colin pressed the buzzer.

"Keep your nose clean until you've done what you came here for."

"No worries" said Leeroy, starting to adopt the slouching posture he had been using when he first entered the room. Rita realised it was all an act for the warder's benefit.

"Great" said Colin, packing up his briefcase and gesturing to Rita that they should leave through the door where the warder was standing.

Rita picked up her coat and bag. She was still puzzled. That interview was nothing like she had imagined it would be. What exactly had just happened?

Thursday 12th September 2019 7.00 pm

The prison alarm was deafening. Warders were appearing on the landings, shepherding inmates to their cells. "Quick as you can, chaps. It's for your safety."

Gary had been in the middle of a table tennis tournament. He had made it to the semi-final. He liked to think this was because of his agility and skill, but he had a suspicion the others might be letting him win, probably because they wanted him to do something. They might want him to get his brother, one of the warders at the prison in Welford Road, to smuggle in more phones, or drugs, or both. He would no doubt get a message soon, even though they were going into a lockdown. The Government and their contractors thought they were running the prison, but the inmates knew differently.

"What's up, Jock?" he asked a Scottish warder who was checking the prisoners went into the right cells.

"Word is, one of the guards has been stabbed to death by a prisoner on remand." he answered. "Christ knows where the weapon came from."

Gary thought he might have a few ideas, but he kept them to himself.

The phone under Gary's mattress was vibrating when he got back to his cell and climbed onto the top bunk. Virat, the occupant of the bottom bunk, took no notice. You learnt to mind your own business in jail. He'd heard there was a ramsey in the prison. He didn't want to know who'd been dipped with it. He went on staring at the pages of a car magazine. Cars had been his downfall since his early teens, and were still an addiction. He couldn't resist stealing wheels. Beamers were best, you could really burn rubber with those. They were so easy to get into these days with electronic keys. A good car fenced away would keep him in drugs for months and there was nothing like the high of racing the feds in a newly nicked car. It was bad luck that, the last time, after he'd been picked up by a traffic cop waiting on the M1, he'd ended up wrapping the BMW 5-series round a tree after he'd roared off the motorway at Hinckley. Before the car hit the tree, that woman and the child she was with had hit the bonnet. People laid flowers at the spot. He'd seen it on the local news.

Virat was supposed to be writing a letter to the woman's partner, to show his contrition, his counsellor said. Virat wasn't sure what that meant, other than that it would be of help with the Parole Board. He didn't want to think about it now. He wanted to look at the cars. He certainly did not want to know what Gary was up to, or anything about the shanking. The less he knew the less he could tell.

"Marty let us down." the voice on the phone was saying into Gary Briggs' ear. "We had to deal with him."

Gary tucked the phone away in its hiding place. Not the best way to learn your brother was dead, he thought. He'd better look out for himself now his brother was gone.

Friday 13th September 2019 11.30am

Three days after the interview in Welford Road prison with Leeroy, Rita was at Leicester Crown Court, in Wellington Street, for the adjourned trial of a client. He had allegedly poured a pot of boiling noodles over his boss in the kitchen of a Chinese restaurant. There were no witnesses to this incident, which was odd, considering how many people seemed to be employed in the kitchen and in front of house roles. According to the client, the owner kept him and his wife in a cramped flat above the restaurant, for which he charged them rent which was only just covered by what the worker could earn. Deductions were made from his pitiful wages for minor mistakes in the kitchen, and he had ended up owing the boss a lot of money, with no hope of repaying the debt. It had all boiled over, literally and metaphorically, when the boss started taking a shine to the client's wife. Rita, and the associate solicitor handling the case, were trying to run a defence of provocation, as this was a one-off, unpremeditated, loss of self-control in a pressurised environment.

What had impeded the progress of the trial had been the absence of an interpreter. Their client spoke poor English, and it was important that he be able to give evidence in his own words, which could be relayed to the jury in English.

Rita had been hoping that Friday 13th would not turn out to be unlucky, but she hoped in vain. The Interpretation Service had once again promised someone who had failed to show, wasting the time of the lawyers and the judge, causing disruption to the court timetable and the allocation of jurors, not to mention the upset to their client and his family. The sooner it could all be dealt with online the better, Rita thought. It would be easier to access an interpreter from China than get one to a court in Leicester.

She had been sitting on a chair, outside Court 2, when she caught sight of Colin Shawcross out of the corner of her eye. Rita had been trying to console the client's wife, who was now 8 months pregnant and anxious that her husband would still be on remand when her baby came. Colin was in the company of a female barrister she had not met before, and Leeroy Roberts, the prisoner she had visited with Colin earlier that week. Everyone was shaking hands as if the proceedings in Court 1, from where they had emerged, had gone well. The barrister swept off her wig as she walked away to the robing room, revealing a head of short blond hair. Colin took Leeroy to the area of chairs where Rita was sitting. He seemed absorbed in what he had to say to Leeroy, and did not notice Rita as he sat with his back to her. Rita carried on smiling sympathetically at Mrs Wong, whose English was worse than her husband's, while managing to overhear what it was that Colin had to impart to Leeroy so urgently.

"You understand what just happened in there and why, yeh?" this did not sound like the way one would usually give a client legal advice, Rita thought.

"You've been bailed for a reason. Here's the details." Rita risked a quick glance. Colin was handing over an envelope, the contents of which made it bulge.

"Do it and I'll get you off this charge altogether." had she heard that right?

Mrs Wong was standing up to go, sobbing into the tissues

Rita had given her. Rita took her arm, steering her carefully through the throng of people waiting for their cases to be called, mindful of the woman's condition and wishing others would take notice too and give her some space. By the time they had made it safely to the door and Rita had prised Mrs Wong into a taxi Rita had forgotten all about the conversation she had overheard.

Chapter

3

"This is my simple religion. There is no need for temples; no need for complicated philosophy. Our own brain, our own heart is our temple; the philosophy is kindness."

Dalai Lama

Friday 27th December 2019 4.30 pm

"What are we going to do? What's happening?" the man Rita had followed into this strange building broke into her recollections. He sounded panicky. As the three of them stood in the entrance of the old factory, Rita's backpack lying between them on the floor, the enigma that was Colin Shawcross was continuing to spring surprises.

"Take her phone!" Colin Shawcross barked to his accomplice just as her mobile, which was in the front pocket of her bag, began to vibrate.

"Put it on loudspeaker!" Colin was still giving the orders.

A voice Rita knew well spoke from the phone. "Hello. This is DCI Jamie Bridge, who am I speaking to?"

"None of your business!" Colin snapped menacingly.

"We heard a gunshot. Can you assure me no one was injured?" Jamie Bridge spoke evenly.

"Yeh" Colin replied sharply. He indicated with his finger to his lips that neither Rita nor the other man were to make a sound. Since Colin had a gun in his hand – something Rita was still finding hard to believe - she thought she had better not disobey.

"A young woman is in your building, is she unharmed?" the voice from the phone asked.

"Yeh." the monosyllabic reply came again. "She's stayin'. We're not comin' out."

"There's no rush. Can we get you anything?" Jamie Bridge tried again.

Rita caught a twinkle in Colin Shawcross's eye. He winked at the other man.

"I dunno." Rita realised Colin was trying to disguise his voice. He was speaking in a lower tone than usual and putting on an Eastenders' accent. "Pizza?" The other man shrugged his shoulders in a form of agreement.

"Yeh. Three pizzas." Colin looked at Rita. "All vegetarian. Vegan if you can. We don't want no animals suffering. Call back when you've got 'em." He cut off the call.

Friday 27th December 2019 4.35 pm

"Upstairs!" Colin Shawcross, her erstwhile boss at the law firm, pointed to a flight of steps next to the cupboard where Rita had been attempting to hide. The man Rita had been following went first, followed by Rita, then Colin, who was waving the gun to encourage her to move. They must make a strange sight, she thought, as she stumbled on uneven steps which were sticky on some of the treads. The place was not well maintained, she concluded.

At the top of the first flight of the stairs, they led her to the left. Their little group entered a room which was long, probably the width of the building Rita guessed, with a tall ceiling to which an ancient fan clung, clogged with cobwebs. It looked like it had not been used in years. The brown linoleum of the corridor floor continued into this room, and the walls were a dirty cream colour. Rita thought, perhaps years of nicotine from people smoking cigarettes in there had soaked into the building. It was as if they had stepped into a sepia photograph. Along the side opposite the door there were high windows so you wouldn't be able to see out unless you stood on something. A strange choice for Colin to make, was Rita's impression, unless he had calculated that if he could not look out then the police could not look in? A large dark-brown wooden counter ran the length of the room under the window and there were marks on it as if it had once held machinery.

The other man pulled up an old wooden chair and gestured for Rita to sit on it. She did so carefully, not sure if the chair was solid enough to take her weight. It had a round seat and a curved back. It looked as old as the building which, as she had entered through the large double wooden door, had looked to date from the last century, some time between the two World Wars, she guessed.

"Tie her up." Colin Shawcross said authoritatively.

Rita's body jolted in shock.

"What?" Rita's quarry sounded perplexed.

"Tie her up while we think what to do. She's brought the cops with her!" Colin indicated with his empty hand the outside of the building, where sirens could still be heard. It was odd that the police had reacted so quickly, Rita was thinking. The surprises were certainly building up today.

Rita looked from one man to the other. She had not expected to encounter them both together, and she had no idea they were acquainted. Then, as her captors stared at one another, probably wondering how this was going to play out, another thought struck her. How well did she know either of them? Initially, as they made her climb the stairs, she thought that recognising them was a good thing. They wouldn't harm someone they knew, would they? Now, as the staring match ended and she was tied to the chair with pieces of rope, she began to think this might have been a miscalculation. Rita's stomach started to churn at the thought of what might happen next, and she wriggled uncomfortably on the old wooden chair. They couldn't keep her here for long, could they?

Rita had been in scrapes before, and the months she had spent in Devon, between leaving uni and starting at the law firm, had not been without incident, but this situation seemed the most dangerous she had ever faced. Colin was unstable at the best of times, and she did not wish to predict what might be the outcome of Colin under pressure with a gun in his hand. Rita tried to breathe deeply and think of something other than the peril she was in.

Her memory of her days at Warwick University, from which she had graduated two years ago, were fading, and being replaced with thoughts of everything that had happened since. When she had finished her history degree, Rita had moved back to her mother's house in Oadby, a few miles from the centre of Leicester, and had concentrated on her Law Conversion Course at Leicester University, while casting around for a suitable firm for a training contract when she moved on to the Legal Practice Course. The Conversion Course had only required two days of contact time, but it had been pretty full-on that year as she grappled with a whole new series of subjects. The seven core subjects were: contract, criminal, European Union, land, public, and tort law, plus equity and trusts. Her eighth subject, which she had chosen, was immigration law.

With that year out of the way, Rita had wanted a break before starting the Practice Course, plus she had to work to fund her internship. She had decided that Morwenna's father's legal firm, in the centre of Leicester, was a good option for her legal training, but it turned out that they wouldn't have a vacancy until summer 2019. The firm covered a range of work, and, once settled there, she could move out of the family home and share a flat with Morwenna, as the friends had planned. It had looked like in the months between completing the Conversion course, and starting at the firm, rather than pursue her career as a solicitor she would have to increase her shifts as a barista at Caffe Nero in the centre of the city. Then came the offer of a few months' work for Athena, Morwenna's mother. It had seemed best to take it up, even if it was in Devon.

Rita tried to control her breathing as she sat on the old chair and to remember what had been happening last autumn to make her glad to leave Leicester after the Law Conversion Course. After all, she could have stayed, but she had wanted to get away. Perhaps it was the sirens, which could still he heard outside the factory, or perhaps it was the promise of pizza, but memories were returning as to why this time last year she had found herself looking forward to helping out at Athena's health food shop and guest house in Totnes. It started with the accident, she recalled.

Saturday 27*th* October 2018 8.30pm

The flat which Rita was planning to share when she started her internship was in Watkin Road, Freemans Meadow, on the west side of Leicester. Still planning to live in the family home, and continue to work at Caffe Nero until the internship began, she had been visiting one evening late in October to check that Morwenna could get someone else to flat share for a few months until Rita could join her. The two young women had been together in the kitchen area helping themselves to pizza when they heard a loud bang.

"That didn't sound good" Morwenna said, shaking her head of bright blonde hair which she was wearing long, almost down to her waist. She was planning to put some curls into it later before she went out with Adam, her current boyfriend. Morwenna had met him while working on a campaign; she was in PR, he was in brand representation.

"No" Rita agreed in a troubled tone. She put down her slice which was oozing hot vegan cheese and walked to her bedroom window so she could see what was happening outside. The full-length window looked out across the river in the direction of the King Power Stadium, the home ground of Leicester City Football Club. The sky was a strange colour, almost like there was a flashing yellow light coming from somewhere. Before she could make out what was causing this effect, her older brother Mohal had called on her mobile.

"Put on Sky Sports sis!!" he yelled instantly and insistently, "Something's happened to the owner's helicopter!"

"Wha..? What do you mean?" Rita stuttered, turning back to the living room and picking up the TV remote in her other hand.

"We will bring you whatever information we can…" the presenter was saying, looking around for details to be relayed to him which he could read out.

"OMG!" Morwenna exclaimed, staring at the screen, her hand going to her mouth in horror.

The two young women, standing frozen in disbelief, had looked at the breaking news message evolving on the screen to understand what was happening a few hundred metres away from the flat. As the full horror struck them, the noise of emergency sirens began to fill the air. The sound was like the mind-numbing shrieks of the howling banshees which Rita's brother, Nayan, had told her about when she had asked about the warrior women figures in his Warhammer game.

Wednesday 7th November 2018 6.00 pm

Rita and her family had set off for the Diwali lights switch-on that year, which took place only a few days after the accident, in a more sombre mood than usual, Rita recalled. It had taken their home town several days to absorb the news of the tragedy. Following the match against West Ham, the helicopter belonging to the club's owner, which had become a familiar sight at Leicester City's home matches, had taken off from the King Power stadium and, almost immediately, plummeted to the ground, becoming engulfed in flames. From the flat that night, she and Morwenna had watched the trails of blue flashing lights as the progress of the emergency services, who were quickly on the scene, cast a ghostly glow on the roads below the flat. Piecing together what they could see, together with the on-the-spot reporting from SKY, where sports journalists were hastily trying to cover a major news event, it seemed that the owner, Vichai Srivaddhanaprabha, and four others on board, had died in the wreckage of the AgustaWestland AW169. Firefighters, police, paramedics, and the Hazardous Area Response team, all of whom had rushed to the scene within two minutes, had been unable to do anything but secure the scene and recover the bodies.

* * *

Over the next few days, the accident had dominated all local news and talk. The football ground became a shrine; a carpet of flowers was laid by distraught fans who queued patiently to pay their respects. Messages of support had been received from other clubs, and throughout the world, the team's unlikely premiership success in 2016 having struck a chord with many people. The owner, Vichai, had been much loved, and stories of his generosity to people in the city were emerging daily. As well as the two pilots, two members of staff had also died. It was a miracle that the helicopter had plunged to earth at a remote part of the car park, and no one on the ground had been injured. Kasper Schmeichel, the goalkeeper, had witnessed the accident. Several people at the site had tried to put out the flames in order to open the helicopter's doors and rescue the occupants, but in vain.

Rita, living back at home with her mother, had found the sadness in the city oppressive. She was also finding her mother's attention a little smothering, and then there was her aunt, Jaina. Her daughters, the twins Shona and Shreya, were about to go on a gap year adventure abroad before they began their university studies. Their itinerary had been planned by Jaina down to the last detail, and their journey would start the day after the Diwali celebrations began. Rita's aunt, always a worrier, had gone into overdrive at the prospect of her daughters disappearing abroad for months. She was at the house of her sister, Padma, most evenings, wailing and worrying. This at least gave her husband, Bandhu, a break, but it added to the strain on Rita. "I don't know how you put up with it." she said to her mother as she played with her muesli at breakfast one day. "Oh, I'm used to it." was Padma's stoical reply. "She won't change. Sure you don't want some fruit juice to drink? Vitamin C is very important for teeth and bones, you know."

When Athena, having heard from Morwenna that Rita might welcome a change, rang to say she needed an operation and was looking for someone to keep the business going while she recuperated, Rita had leapt at the chance. She could have a room in the guest house, Athena told her. She, Athena, would do the ordering of stock for the shop. Rita would just need to price it up and sell it. There were lots of loyal customers in Totnes itself, Athena told her enthusiastically, as well as visitors to the town, and the guests, who were fewer in number in the winter months. Athena said she would simplify the breakfast on offer while she was incapacitated, having regard to Rita's culinary abilities, or lack of them. Athena would be having a hysterectomy in a few weeks' time, she told Rita, and would be out of action until well after Christmas. She had been advised in particular not to do any lifting for a few weeks.

"That's ok" Rita said brightly, "I can look after you, as well, provided you stock up the freezer with meals for us."

"Deal" said Athena and Rita's course for the next few months had been set.

The switch-on of over 6,000 lights on the 'Golden Mile' on Belgrave Road in Leicester took place at 7.30 pm. With thousands attending, Rita and her family, in keeping with tradition, had got there early to take in the atmosphere and look at the food stalls, despite Padma's warnings not to spoil their appetites for the meal she had prepared for them back at home. This meal was billed as a 'farewell to Rita', even though she had assured her mother that Totnes was not abroad, only four hours away by car, and that members of the family would be welcome to stay at the guest house for free, as Athena had promised. The switch-on ended, as it did every year, with a spectacular firework display which could be seen from miles away and which they all drank in, uttering gasps with the rest of the crowd at the magnificence of it.

Earlier, Shreya and Shona, Rita's twin cousins, together with Nayan, had left the family group to take in the excitement of the fun fair set up as part of the celebrations, and to ride on the big wheel, known as the Wheel of Light. Mohal joined them once he had added an item to his vlog about the helicopter crash and its effect on the City. Rita had stayed by her mother's side, in view of Padma's concern at her leaving, and together they had commented on the Indian dancing and other entertainments provided, standing with their arms linked together, their round faces and heads of curly hair bending towards one another.

Eventually the group made their way back to the Haymarket car park where Bandhu, Jaina's husband, picked up his family, and where Mohal and Mahir had also left their cars. They drove in convoy back to 10 Elm Drive in Oadby, Rita and Padma with Mahir, Nayan with his brother. At the meal, Jaina insisted on listing what might go wrong for Shona and Shreya on their travels, and all the medicines she had packed in their cases. Rita wondered if they would be able to keep a straight face when asked at the airport who had packed their luggage. "You are lucky, Rita is staying in the country and will be with a good friend." Jaina said to justify her concerns.

Shona and Shreya smiled benignly at their mother and whispered conspiratorially when out of her earshot. They were not the innocents that her aunt liked to think, in Rita's experience. Eighteen months ago now, when they were supposed to be studying for their A levels, she had come across them in a wine bar in the city centre. What had made the encounter even more memorable was that one of them had been very familiar with Jai, the brother-in-law of her best friend, Priya. At the time, Rita had been unsure whether to tell anyone, but had decided against. Hearing about the twins trip abroad, it suggested the affair was over, she had concluded.

"Perhaps the children and I can visit you over the Christmas break?" Mahir had quietly asked as he passed Rita a bowl of sag aloo, one of her mother's specialities.

"Yes, that would be lovely." Rita said. "You can all stay at the guest house." Missing Mahir had been the one downside to helping out Athena. Rita had thought hard about it, but decided she should not turn down the opportunity. Besides, it was only for a few months and, after that, they could have more time together as she gathered experience at the law firm and prepared for her Legal Practice exam. There was plenty of time, she thought. They could keep in touch through Skype and Snapchat, but it would be great to know she was actually going to see him in December. The children had been very young when their mother was tragically killed, in her own home, by burglars. They needed to be with their father whenever possible, she understood that. Perhaps if the weather was good when they visited, they could drive to one of the local beaches where there would be lots for Sadhil and Aashi to enjoy, even in winter.

"I hope you won't try anything stupid, Rita." She was startled from the memories she had been indulging in by a voice in her ear. The other man, the one she had been following, was crouching close while Colin was across the room, apparently barking orders into his phone. Rita puzzled for a second as to who the lawyer could be talking to. Then she moved her gaze back to the other man. She had had suspicions about him for some time, she realised, not least this time last year when she had stumbled across him by chance while she was in Devon.

Chapter

4

"I prefer painting people's eyes to cathedrals, for there is something in the eyes that is not in the cathedral, however solemn and imposing the latter may be — a human soul, be it that of a poor beggar or of a street walker, is more interesting to me."

Vincent van Gogh

Friday 7th December 2018 5.00 pm

It was just over a year ago that she had arrived in Totnes. Rita had enjoyed the relaxing nature of Athena's company after the intensity of her mother and aunt at home in Leicester. The older woman showed her what needed to be done at the Devon B&B during the weeks they had together, until the time came for her operation at the Derriford hospital in Plymouth. Rita had taken her there, and collected her when she was discharged. The hardest thing about the weeks following had been to make sure that Athena recovered, and did not try to do too much. Morwenna, Athena's daughter and Rita's flatmate- to- be, called by a couple of times before Christmas, but her presence was more of a hindrance than a help, Rita found, as she seemed to expect to be looked after as a guest. Rita hoped Morwenna's attitude would change when they were living together.

"I must look a fright!" Athena had said in the car on their way back from the hospital to the guest house in Totnes. Her hair, dyed auburn, was shoulder length and tied in a pony tail from which tails of loose hair trailed. She had no make-up, which leant her a pale look, and her usual flamboyant earrings had been left at home.

"We'll soon get you straight." Rita had said tactfully. "One step at a time."

"You sound like me!" Athena said, brightening up, "I'm glad a little of my philosophy is rubbing off on you. Or is it working in the health food shop?"

"I expect it's both!" Rita laughed, thinking how easily she had settled into Athena's routine of getting up at 6am to set the table for the guests' breakfast, eating her own muesli on the go as she did so. Breakfast was a continental one, with fresh fruit and organic yoghurts accompanying a variety of breads from a nearby bakery, and locally sourced jam and honey. Many of the guests were walkers, there to explore the local moors, and they had good appetites. Other guests preferred to visit the seaside resorts in the vicinity ,and the independent shops, of which Totnes had an abundance. Once breakfast was over, Rita's job was to supervise the cleaner in tidying the kitchen and cleaning the rooms, while keeping any eye on the health food shop. She usually had time for a mint tea or two when sitting by the till, and on quiet days could even fit in a bit of reading, although it was common to find that, as soon as she opened her book, a customer would walk in.

She looked in on Athena at lunchtime to make her report, and check her boss had everything she needed. Athena was keen to help and had to be restrained. Rita got used to being economical with the truth, especially when the cleaner was ill and Rita had to do her tasks herself. One thing Rita was grateful for was that the meditation workshops, which Athena usually ran, had been taken over by a lady called Corina who sported a leopard skin patterned headband and a matching yoga leotard. She and her acolytes took over the lounge three mornings and three evenings a week but, as their practice was silent, they were no trouble, provided the cleaner and the guests kept out of their way.

In a couple of weeks, Athena was managing better and she and Rita had enjoyed a nut roast together on Christmas day. The guest house and shop were closed and, on Boxing Day, Mahir came with his offspring for their promised visit. The children had been fractious and tired after the long drive when they arrived, so Rita's idea of a cosy evening with Mahir while the little ones lay sleeping in their beds did not go to plan. They asked for pizza to eat, although Rita had defrosted a vegetable pie for them to share. She dug pizzas out of the freezer and put them in the oven, but by the time they were ready Aashi and Sadhil were saying they wanted baked beans.

Mahir offered to heat up beans and the four of them finally settled together on the sofas in the guest house sitting room. Mercifully, the meditation sessions were suspended for the holidays. They had a Disney film on DVD to watch and bowls of pizza, pie and beans to eat. It was different she supposed. The children had eventually succumbed to sleep as the film ended and, after Mahir had carted them upstairs and got them settled in the family room, which the three of them would be sharing, he returned, and he and Rita could greet each other properly at last.

"I'm sorry" he said after a while, "They are a handful."

"They're your handful, so I like them." Rita replied. "What shall we do with them tomorrow?"

Thursday 27th December 2018 10.00 am

After a breakfast of toast with jam, and chocolate almond milk, a variation on the usual guest house meal, Rita and Mahir took the children to Dawlish Warren, about a half hour drive. Athena suggested this was likely to have attractions open for children at this time of year, and she had been proved right. First, with views of the red sandstone cliffs, which were a distinctive feature of the coast there, they walked along the sandy beach for quite a while, the weather being sunny and bright if not warm. They collected stones and shells, which they carried to the car in an old bucket they found by the shore. After that, there was time for fairground rides and arcade games, which Aashi and Sadhil threw themselves into with enthusiasm. They lunched on fish and chips before driving to Dawlish. The coastline here was stunning, and Rita would have liked it if they could have travelled on the train. The Riviera line between Exeter and Paignton was one of the most scenic in the country. But being the Christmas break there were no trains running.

Dawlish itself was a small town. It had its own beach and they walked along it, and then on the seafront road to the small shops and cafes. These were arranged around an open park area through which ran a small stream with swans on it. The children played with a football for a while, allowing another child who was passing to join in. The late evening sun was starting to set as they left a café in Dawlish, replete with tea, lemonade and scones. Sadhil and Aashi inevitably fell asleep on the back seat as they drove to the guest house, where Athena had warmed up a vegetable lasagne. "It's going to be another long evening!" Mahir had observed and Rita laughed.

* * *

The children finally gave in to sleep again at about 10 pm. Rita had dozed off on the sofa by then, and hardly noticed when Mahir scooped them up and took them out of the sitting room. When he returned, he kissed Rita gently and helped her out of the chair. Fresh air and keeping any eye on two lively children had really taken it out of her. She just wasn't used to it.

"Come on, sleepy head." he said. "Tomorrow's forecast isn't so good. The kids want to go to the cinema, so I thought I'd take them to Exeter. You don't have to come if you've had enough" he added generously.

"Oh no, I'll come for the ride." Rita said, stretching and yawning rather dramatically "Maybe I'll have some 'me' time in Exeter while you're watching the movie and we can eat together afterwards? There's lots of places there that the children would like."

Friday 28th December 2018 11 am

So, the scheme for the next day had taken shape. The small boy and girl, in their matching white padded jackets and trousers, had to be installed on their car seats. They were wearing earphones so they could play their computer games. They looked like miniature astronauts, Rita thought, ready for the rocket launch. The in-car entertainment kept them quiet all the way to Exeter, however, so Mahir and Rita could talk freely. He said how much he was missing her, and that he might be able to get down to Totnes at the end of January. There was a dental conference in Plymouth he could attend, if Padma was willing. Rita said she would work on her mother, and mused aloud when she might be able to take a few days off from helping Athena and pop back to Leicester. "It'll be more like March, I would think," she told Mahir. Although Athena was making a good recovery, she ought not to be taking on the heavy lifting and rushing around that the guest house and the shop demanded. Her aim was to be back to full capacity by Easter, when business really started to pick up.

"Maybe we can come down again at the February half term?" Mahir offered. Rita looked at the small figures in the back of the car absorbed in their screens. "Yes" she said, "that would be nice". She had grown fond of the little ones, even though they could be a nightmare at times.

It rained all the way on their trip to Exeter, but fortuitously it stopped just as they arrived. Rita left Mahir and his progeny at the Vue cinema. They were going to see Mary Poppins Returns. (Where is she when you need her? Rita had smiled to herself). Rita set off for the Cathedral. She liked to walk around the green which was overlooked by the imposing building, with its twin Norman towers, construction having commenced in 1114, although the first cathedral on the site had been founded by Edward the Confessor in 1050. It was often a lively part of the city, with people using the paths across the Green to get to other quarters of the town. Fairs and entertainments were held there and it was the meeting point for the red coat guides who led daily walking tours of various parts of Exeter. Today, because it was a holiday, and because of the weather, it was fairly quiet, with just a few cathedral visitors walking through.

Rita decided to set off for Queen Street, hoping the Royal Albert Memorial Museum would be open; after the museums in Leicester, it was one of her favourites. There was always something new to find in history she found. She crossed the road to Southernhay, a wide street with grass and trees dividing the cars from each other and lined with Georgian-style houses, then she turned into a lane leading to the cathedral. As she walked along, Exeter Cathedral School was on her left. Ahead of her she could see the medieval façade of Mol's Coffee House. The building had seen many uses over the years, Rita knew. The Royal Coat of Arms on the front was in recognition of its role as a Customs House in the 16th century, until the opening of the Customs House on Exeter Quay. It then became successively an apothecary, a shoe shop and a haberdashery until the coffee shop was opened in the 18th century. Mol was a shortened form of Mary, and in fact the coffee shop had been run by different women for practically a hundred years, Rita had discovered. It had ceased to be a coffee house in 1837, put out of business by the competition. As Rita got nearer, she could see the hoardings beside the alleyway which led from the green to High Street. They were an ugly reminder of the fire in October 2016 that had destroyed the Royal Clarence Hotel, built in 1769 as the Assembly Rooms. Its façade was a great loss to the green and it was unclear whether it would be restored to anything like its former glory.

Rita was lost in thought, thinking of the murder which had taken place near the cathedral in November 1283. A student of history, the story of the murder had caught her attention. The victim was the precentor of the cathedral, that was the person who led the singing, as she understood it. He had been set upon by a mob in the area near the cathedral now occupied by the school. The attack was the result of rivalry for power between the city's guilds and the cathedral authorities. Twenty-one people, including the Dean and the Mayor, were charged with involvement in the conspiracy. The trial was conducted by King Edward 1 himself, such was its perceived importance. The hearing took place in the Great Hall of Exeter Castle. Only ruins of the castle, otherwise known as Rougemont, survived, Rita knew. They stood against the skyline in gardens between the museum and the Central Library. She might be able to walk through the gardens on her way to meet Mahir and his offspring.

In all, five men were executed for the murder. The Dean had claimed his right to be tried by the church authorities and, not surprisingly, he was found not guilty. The Crown had sided with the Church, and the two main institutions of medieval England had protected each other against the guild members. Rita was so absorbed in remembering this incident, she almost bumped into someone on the path. He was coming towards her rather quickly, and was past her in a flash, but she had registered various things about him. He was taller than she was, wearing a yellow padded jacket, and had a distinctive earring in his right ear. The reason he had made such a strong impression on her, although they had passed each other so quickly, was that Rita knew him.

It was Jai Choudhrie, brother-in-law of her best friend Priya and married to Priya's sister Meera. He was a lecturer at Loughborough University but had taken a sabbatical from his teaching duties, the last she heard. Could he still be on sabbatical? Rita wondered. She had no idea how long was allowed for those breaks. Meera had said something about a grant to look into the Chinese economy? Maybe he was writing a book? When Rita had seen him previously, he had been in a wine bar in Leicester in the company of her twin cousins, and looked very close to one of them, Shona. There was something not right about him, Rita had thought. All ideas of museums and castles abandoned, she had turned on her heels and trailed after Jai.

Rita had tracked Jai carefully. He was easy to follow in his yellow jacket, which made him stand out among the few people who were out strolling, enjoying the break in the rain. He unwittingly led her down Southernhay and across Magdalen Street into Colleton Crescent. From there, Exeter Quay could be seen below. Rita did not have time to look at the view, however. Jai had put what looked like a supermarket carrier bag into a waste bin, and was waiting by the side of the road. Rita hid behind a tree to watch. Fairly soon, a red Mazda MX-5 Convertible drew up. He exchanged words with the driver, a dark-haired man of about 30 with a full black beard. Then he got in and the car sped off. Rita made a note of the registration, extracted herself from her hiding place, and went over to look in the waste bin, putting her gloves on first. The bag was an orange one from Sainsburys. It had been folded up. Rita slowly unwound it and tried to open it at the handles, although it seemed there was something sticky inside making this difficult. Fortunately, there was no one about to witness her suspicious behaviour, although figures could be seen below enjoying a walk by the quayside. Finally, the sides of the bag gave way to her efforts. Rita could see what the problem had been. Inside was a sticky dark red substance. She was fairly sure it was blood. Hastily, she folded the bag up again and dropped it back in the bin. It was time to find out what Mary Poppins had been doing.

Friday 28th December 2018 3.00 pm

The children had enjoyed the film and regaled Rita with tales of what had happened in it while they sat together in Pizza Express, overlooking Cathedral Green, where Rita had seen Jai not that long before. Rita was not paying much attention. She was looking out of the window. It seemed there was an on-going incident at the cathedral. The police had taped off the main entrance, on the west side, and the only people going in appeared to be police officers, not clergy, visitors or worshippers.

"I wonder what's going on there?" she said idly as she helped herself to the salad they were all sharing.

"Leave it, Rita!" Mahir's apparent attempt to admonish her was spoilt by his smile, "You can't solve all the world's mysteries, you know." he grinned.

Rita smiled back. She thought it best not to mention that she had seen Jai. He couldn't be involved in whatever was going on, surely?

Before they went back to the car, which was parked in Princesshay, the main shopping centre of the city, Rita got her wish. They took Sahil and Aashi to the ruins of Rougemont Castle, built by the Normans to protect Exeter, which was well fortified by walls begun in Roman times, when the city was called Isca Dumnoniorum. The two children scrambled over the ruins and ran around in the surrounding park and gardens until it got too dark. Surprisingly, both children stayed awake on the drive back to Totnes this time. Athena had kindly prepared an indoor picnic for Aashi and Sadhil and offered to sit with them while Mahir and Rita had some time together.

Later, when Mahir was tucking his children into bed, Athena had been sitting on the sofa, watching while Rita cleared away the remains of the picnic.

"Cheers for that." Rita said, "It was really kind of you."

"It was the least I could do, after all you've done for me." Athena replied, "Actually, something odd happened while you were in Exeter today." Athena added.

"Oh?" Rita was curious. "Anything to do with the cathedral?"

"How did you know?" Athena responded. "You haven't been getting involved in anything have you?"

"No, of course not." Rita replied, not looking her in the eye. "We saw some police at the cathedral, while we were at Pizza Express, that's all." she explained.

"It was on the local news. Someone left a person's head in there." Athena went on.

"What?" Rita stopped clearing up, astonished at what Athena had said.

Athena shrugged. "Just like I said. Who knows whose it is, or why it was left there?"

Friday 27th December 2019 8.00 pm

This incident played through Rita's mind as the man, the one she had followed into the factory building, crouched next to her and whispered a warning into her ear. He was so close that his earring almost touched her cheek. It was very distinctive. Rita would recognise it anywhere. It was the earring that Meera had bought her new husband on their safari honeymoon. The man Rita had followed into this dangerous situation was the man she had followed in Exeter that day. It was Jai. What was he involved in? And how did he know Colin? Rita struggled to make sense of it all.

Chapter

5

"The Christian catacombs represent simplicity and earthiness; the cathedrals, transcendence and wonder."
Russell Moore

Friday 27th December 2019 8.00 pm

In the strange room, in the disused hosiery factory, Rita was still sitting on the funny chair, her bum going numb. Her hands had been freed, so she could tuck into the pizza, but her legs remained tied to the legs of the chair. She had not been all that hungry. She had watched the men tuck in with enthusiasm.

"I need the bathroom." Rita announced after a while, looking forward to having her legs released. They were starting to go numb, too.

"Oh, OK" typical of Colin not to have realised this situation would arise. His planning skills in the office had not been much better.

Colin picked up his own phone, not Rita's, and sent a message.

"Won't be long." he said casually.

While she waited, Rita wondered what was happening outside the building. The sirens had ceased a while ago. Presumably the police were watching. Did they have any cameras or surveillance equipment inside, she wondered? They seemed to be taking Colin and Jai seriously. The pizzas had not been a ploy for the police to storm the building, as she had, for a brief moment, hoped. They had been left, as agreed, outside the front door. Someone, not Colin or the other man, must have taken them in, because the two men had been in the room with her when a third person, who Rita could not see, came to the door of the room and handed them in.

So, there was at least one other person in the building, and the way Colin was sending messages and shouting orders on his phone she began to wonder if there were several other people there, or in the vicinity. There seemed to be an urgency about what he wanted them to do. Who were these people? Even more of a mystery was, why they were at Colin's beck and call. He did not command much authority at work.

After her request for the loo, Rita was about to find out the identity of the third person in the building. A woman in her late thirties, with curly black hair sprouting under a baseball cap, came into the room. She was wearing red dungarees over an orange jumper. Rita knew her. It was Anya, Colin's wife. Rita had done some babysitting for them. Things were taking a very strange turn.

"You need the loo, Rita?" she asked as if they were just socialising together.

"Go with Anya." Colin ordered, "I'll be right behind so don't try anything." he added, making it clear this was no ordinary occasion.

The bathroom visit took all of ten minutes, however much Rita tried to stretch it out. There was a communal toilet a few metres down from the room. Anya waited outside the cubicle door, while Colin stayed in the corridor. It was not exactly relaxing, Rita thought. But it was good to be able to move around a bit, and she rubbed her ankles to get the circulation back. Then she went to the sink, hoping to warm her hands under the tap, but the water was cold, so she settled for washing them thoroughly, and wiping them on a paper towel.

"Don't milk it." Anya said, with a cold look in her eye that Rita had never seen before. "Let's go."

Anya and her husband escorted Rita back to the room

and this time Anya tied her to the chair. She had lost track of time. It seemed to have gone dark outside. How long did they intend to keep her here? She did not fancy spending the night on this chair, but it looked very much as if she was going to have to.

It was odd that Anya was clearly not fazed by Colin waving a gun around. Rita felt like she was having one of those dreams where random people turn up in surreal situations and no one questions it. Anya seemed very composed, more in control of herself than her husband, in fact. When she had first met Anya, Rita remembered, she had been anything but calm.

Monday 18th November 2019 10.30 am

A few months into her internship, and Rita was still working in the Criminal Department, although she was even more anxious to move. The week had started badly. Rita found herself dragged by Colin Shawcross to the police station on Hinckley Road. Rita had been there once before. It seemed a long time since she had been interviewed at the station by two police officers. It had been very distressing. She wondered if any of the officers would recognise her, or she them. She hoped not. Rita was lucky, staff turnover was high. Officers left the force frequently, citing stress or unsociable hours. Others went to join security firms where the work was less regular but less dangerous too. Better to be guarding a shipping container all day than trying to arrest someone armed with a knife, or high on drugs, or pursuing a motorbike at high speed when the suspect has just poured acid over someone. Even with the increased authorisation for tasers, it was hard to feel safe. It was supposed to be policing by consent. That's what they were told in basic training her brother Nayan, who had looked into these things, had told her. But there was precious little sign of consent on the front line.

Their client was Hardiq Patel. Rita did not know him, but Colin seemed to.

"Hi Hardiq" he greeted him. "I'm sitting in on your interview with the police. I can stop it at any time and we can have a chat, yeh?" Colin Shawcross made eye contact with Hardiq and the two police officers, both women, in the room. Rita took out her iPad.

"This is Miss Patel. She's training with us." Colin explained, downgrading Rita's involvement. "She'll take some notes." Rita's role diminished further. She felt the police officers losing any respect for her they might have had.

"You're being interviewed as a witness?" Colin's voice rose to indicate a question, which he addressed to the officers. Everybody but Rita nodded.

"And you've not been cautioned?" Everyone nodded again. Rita wrote these facts down.

It was interesting in itself, she thought; not many people requested to have legal representation when being interviewed as a witness.

"Thanks for cooperating, Mr Patel" the more senior of the officers was saying, although they both looked quite young, not much older than she was, Rita thought. One had a round face with freckles and short dark hair, the other one was older, and quite thin, with red hair framing a bony face and a way of pursing her lips together whenever the witness spoke, which made it seem she didn't believe him.

"This is about an incident that took place in the Regent Street area of the City. You work at the Seven/Eleven not far from the corner with London Road, I understand."

Hardiq Patel looked sideways at Colin. Rita was able to observe this because she was sitting in a corner of the room behind them. There was no space for her at the table. Colin nodded.

"Yes" Hardiq said.

"And you were working there at 11 pm on Friday 20 September at about half past eleven in the evening?" Hardiq looked at Colin again. "Yes" he said.

"Did you see anything unusual that evening?"

Hardiq looked towards Colin who raised his eyebrows.

"I..I saw a fire."

"OK" the officer with dark hair said in a tone that indicated they were getting somewhere at last.

"And where was this fire?"

"At the house opposite the shop. On the other side of the road," Hardiq spoke quickly now, as if Colin's eyebrows had given him permission.

"And did you see anyone acting suspiciously before the fire?"

Hardiq took a brief glance in Colin's direction. Colin gave an almost imperceptible shake of his head. If Rita had not been sitting behind them both, she might not have noticed it.

"N..no" he said. "I don't know no one." he added.

"No one hanging around the shop who you hadn't seen before, perhaps? Or checking out the houses across the road?"

Colin sat back in his chair and spread out the four fingers and thumb of his right hand on the interview table.

"No." Hardiq sounded quite vehement about this. "I don't see no one."

Rita, writing down these exchanges, was increasingly aware of Colin Shawcross's body language. Had the police officers not picked up on it? she wondered. They did seem focussed on Hardiq, and were not really looking at Colin, she thought. She looked back at her notes while the officers prepared their next question.

What date did they say the fire was? Friday 20 September. Regent Street. Wasn't that when…? Rita's whole body went hot and cold in quick succession. This was the night of the hen party, this was the fire they had come across, surely?

Should she say something? The stern look on Colin's face as he stared at Hardiq suggested that would not be wise. Anyway, the police at the scene had taken her details. If they thought she knew anything they would ask her, surely?

"What happened to the CCTV, Hardiq?" the red-haired Detective Sergeant asked sharply, studying Hardiq's face for a response. Hardiq jumped a little in his seat. Colin raised and lowered his hand which was still spread out on the table, and also stared at his client.

"I..I don't know. It usually works. On that night.. I don't know.." the witness's voice petered out.

"You didn't interfere with it?" the younger Detective Constable asked this time.

Hardiq did not need to look at Colin to answer that one. "I..no." he replied.

"Sounds like you know someone who did?" the Detective Sergeant took up the interrogation again.

In case they had forgotten he was there, Colin interjected, "Can I remind you that my client is being interviewed as a witness." he said firmly, leaning across the table with his hands together, fingers steepled and pointing towards the officers. "Any more accusations and I'll advise him not to cooperate."

The DC coughed. "I don't want to have to investigate you," the DS said, catching Colin's warning eye, "As far as you are aware, did anyone interfere with the recording on the CCTV?" she asked the witness.

Hardiq looked at the table, then looked at the fingers of Colin's right hand which he had once again spread on the top of the table.

"No" he said simply.

"And there's nothing more you can tell us about how the fire started?"

"No." Hardiq answered again.

"What first drew your attention to what was happening

in the house?" the Detective Constable was like a dog with a bone. "Was there a smell of smoke perhaps? Or the sound of an explosion?"

Colin's fingers started to tap on the table.

"Flames. I just saw flames." Hardiq's voice was trembling.

"I went into the back room to call the fire brigade." he added, without looking at Colin, who stirred uneasily in his chair, lifted his hand from the table, and put it down again slowly.

"Really?" the Detective Sergeant took over again, "Wasn't that an odd thing to do?"

Colin leant forward, both hands on the table this time. "I think we agreed that Mr Patel is here to help you, Detective Sergeant." he said, "He can only tell you what happened from his perspective. It's not for you to infer anything from his behaviour. He is a witness not a suspect."

The Detective Sergeant stared back at Colin cynically, pursing her lips, as if to say "for now".

"Sorry." she apologised to Hardiq, "It's just that I am puzzled. You have a mobile phone, yes?"

"Yes" Hardiq admitted.

"And yet, rather than watch the progress of the fire from your shop and relay it to the call handler from your mobile phone, when you decided to notify the fire brigade, you chose to use the landline in the backroom. Where you couldn't see what was happening. And by the time you made the call the fire brigade had been alerted anyway."

Was that us? Rita was thinking. They had seen no one in the vicinity and, as she thought back, she seemed to remember the shop had looked closed, but that might be the benefit of hindsight. She could not be absolutely sure she had noticed the shop at all. A great witness she would make!

Hardiq and Colin exchanged glances. "No credit." Hardiq said.

Colin looked satisfied and took his hand off the table

altogether.

"I think my client has told you all he knows." he said.

Turning to Hardiq Patel, Colin added, "We should go."

Rita rapidly stuffed her iPad into her backpack as she tumbled out of the interview room in Colin's wake. What on earth had that been all about? she wondered. But Rita had no time to speculate about the interview. As they walked through the automatic glass doors at the police station, and Colin said goodbye to Hardiq, giving him an envelope in the process, Colin's phone rang. Rita was near enough to gather it was a personal call. The person on the other end sounded to be in great distress.

Chapter

6

"I looked in temples churches and mosques, But I found the Divine within my heart"

Rumi

Monday 18th November 2019 11.45 am

"You'll have to come to my house" Colin had said when the sobbing phone call had ended.

"I have to go straight there now. You heard what a state she's in." he referred to his wife, "And you might be useful looking after the children." he added.

Oh great, Rita thought, I'm trying to get legal experience and I end up babysitting! But she could not object.

When the taxi drew up outside the police station, Colin gave the driver directions to his home. This turned out to be a detached property occupying a substantial corner plot in a quiet cul-de-sac in Great Glen, about 7 miles from Leicester. Rita did her best not to look impressed. There must be 5 or 6 bedrooms, she thought, counting the upstairs windows she could see, including the dormer window above the double garage. A red Mazda MX-5 was parked on the drive, next to an imposing dark blue BMW. Rita thought the registration plate looked familiar. An immaculate lawn lay to the front of the large bay window next to the front door. The door opened as the taxi pulled up on the driveway. A thin woman with a sharp face and shoulder length curly black hair came running out of the door towards Colin, her hooped earrings swinging when she threw herself at him. Her face was wet with tears as she buried it in Colin's not very substantial chest. Rita climbed out of the car after him. Putting down his briefcase, Colin managed to pay the driver with one hand while comforting the woman, who Rita took to be his wife, with the other.

As the three of them entered the wide hall, off which there was a sweeping wooden staircase to the upper floors, Rita caught sight of a massive family kitchen which her mother would have envied. The kitchen area had two double ovens, a double sink and a large array of cupboards and gadgets. Beyond an imposing island were a large table and chairs, as well as a couple of armchairs. The whole room, which stretched for most of the width of the house, was decked in white and pale blue.

Colin's wife led them, not to the kitchen at the back, but to the living room to the left, the room which had the large bay window visible from the road. Table lamps were reflected in the glass-topped side tables which were scattered between cream leather chairs and sofas, giving the room the air of a hotel lounge, Rita felt, except for the wall mounted TV and family photos, which were the digital sort that kept changing every so often. Rita wondered what Anya did for a living, surely Colin could not afford all this on his associate solicitor salary?

Another dark-haired woman was already in the room, sufficiently similar in appearance to Colin's wife, but younger, for Rita to guess this must be her sister. The other woman was sitting very still and she barely registered their presence as they entered through the glazed door. Two children were seated on the rug in the middle of the room, looking at a cartoon on an iPad. They reminded Rita of Mahir's offspring, they looked similar in age. They had dark hair and sharp features, like their mother, rather than Colin's more mousy appearance. They also did not stir when the group came into the room, but continued to look at the film.

Colin made swift introductions, and started telling people what to do, although no one took any notice of him at first. It was just like being at work, Rita thought.

"Rita, this is Anya, my wife," he had said, indicating the woman from whom he was disentangling himself, "Sonya, her sister," he nodded, with a sympathetic look on his face, towards the woman on the sofa, "and these are Sophia and Alexander, my children." Rita noticed he said 'my' not 'our', typical of Colin.

"Anya, perhaps some tea? Children, go to the playroom please! Rita will come with you."

For about half a minute nothing in the room changed. Colin clapped his hands, as if the only problem was that no one was paying attention. He tried again, "Sophie darling" he spoke to the little girl who looked to be the older of the two, "Would you show Rita the playroom please?" then, turning to Rita, "Would you mind taking the children out? This is a very upsetting time."

"Of course," Rita said, not sure she had a choice, "Come on!" she tucked the iPad under her arm and took the boy and girl by the hand, following Sophia's directions to the playroom which adjoined the living room via a sliding door. Rita left the door slightly open, partly so she could be seen, after all she did not know the children, nor they her, and partly so she could listen to what was happening. This was made easier by the fact that, once Sophia had operated the iPad, the two children were happily watching their cartoon again. They seemed easily occupied, Rita thought.

"Who would do such a thing?" Anya's sister was saying. "The police, they ask did he have any enemies? Had anyone threatened him? I tell them no. He was good husband. He run good business. No trouble."

"I know" she heard Colin say emolliently, trying to reduce the emotional temperature in the room.

"Anya, make us some tea, would you?" he suggested again, but more forcefully. "Sonya, you must stay with us as long as you like. It's a dreadful business, dreadful."

A long sob forced its way out of Sonya.

"When will they let me see him?" she asked her brother-in-law.

"It will probably not be for a couple of days." Colin told her. "Until they've finished their tests." Rita noticed he didn't use the words 'Post Mortem', probably out of a delicacy of feeling towards Sonya.

"My mother, she will come." Sonya said.

"Oh good, good idea." Colin sounded less than enthusiastic. Three Polish women in the house sounded a handful, Rita thought. "She can stay too." he added, unable to make himself sound keen at the idea.

"I can't..I can't.." Sonya made a gulping noise. "I can't make plans. I can't think. I don't know what will happen."

"That's the shock." said Colin.

"Have your drink, then go for a lie down." Anya had encouraged her sister as she came back into the room. Rita could hear cups rattling on a metal tray. It did not seem that Colin's wife had made any tea for her. "We've all had a terrible shock." Anya added.

"What exactly did happen?" Colin asked. Rita was not sure this was tactful.

His wife, Anya, answered. She seemed to have regained control of herself while in the kitchen.

"All we know is that he was at Lidl, the one on Fosse Road North." she spoke slowly. There was the sound of cups being lifted from saucers and then replaced. Anya went on, "He was in the car park when he was stabbed. A passer-by saw him and called an ambulance. A doctor who was just parking there tried to help him. But it was no good."

Sonya let out a sharp gasp. There was the sound of tissues being torn out of a box. Presumably, her tears were flowing now.

"It sounds like a random attack by a stranger." Colin summarised, after a pause. "Wrong place. Wrong time." he sighed "You do read about such things."

Sonya continued to sob, but more quietly, her wet face pressed against her sister's shoulder, as Rita could see through the gap in the sliding door.

"No one saw who did it? What happened to them?" Colin asked. It was like he was in court, Rita thought, examining a witness. Maybe at times of stress it was easier to revert to your professional role, she thought.

"They must have run off." Anya said, speaking over the top of Sonya's head. "The police are searching the area for him – I assume it was a man- and for the knife."

Knife crime was so common nowadays, Rita thought to herself, looking down on Sophia and Alexander, who were oblivious to the evil event which had occurred to their uncle. It was at record levels and no one seemed to know what to do about it. The stop and search powers that had been reintroduced did not seem to have had any effect. Now, a company was producing kitchen knives without sharp points which was a nice idea, but some of the weapons wielded went far beyond the kitchen knife. Machetes were on the increase, too, according to news reports. Mohal, Rita's older brother, had done a vlog about it. A lot of it was related to gangs, he had said, with rival members battling to protect their 'turf', and this included drug dealers who tried to protect their 'patch' from other dealers.

"CCTV?" Colin continued his interrogation.

"No." this time Sonya spoke, "No cameras where James was found. The police hope someone's dashcam might have caught something.." her voice broke at this point and there was the sound of energetic nose blowing.

"I'm bored." Sophia suddenly said, standing up. "Can we go back to Mummy and Daddy now?"

"Come through here." Colin told the trio. "Aunty Sonya's just going to have a rest." he said as the two sisters could be seen leaving the room, their arms around one another.

"Play with Elsa" he said, picking up a doll with long golden hair and dressed in blue; Rita recognised the character from the film Frozen, "and you can play with your cars." He added as he gave Alexander a box of toy Porsches. Colin was clearly no fan of gender-neutral toys, Rita observed.

While the children played as directed, Rita's boss reached for the remote and switched on the large wall-mounted tv, finding a channel with an item about the stabbing. He turned the sound down while he and Rita read the breaking news as it processed across the bottom of the screen.

"Another knife death in Leicester. A man in his late twenties was stabbed in a supermarket car park. The suspect escaped. Police have warned the public not to tackle him." Above the words, there appeared film of the branch of Lidl on Fosse Road North. Rita knew it well. Police tape had sealed off the shop, and the car park, and there was a reporter standing across the road, pointing out the corner of the car park where the incident had happened. This was followed by a longer camera shot of the surrounding area, presumably to indicate the direction which the culprit might have taken, and then a still photo of a smiling man standing next to Sonya on their wedding day.

It was all Rita could do not to shout out in alarm. She knew that face! She had seen him before. Rita was certain that he was the bearded man who had picked up Jai when she had followed him in Exeter last year, and she had seen him with Jai in Durham only a week or so ago. What business did he have there? Why had he died in an apparently random attack? At the time Rita had decided this was not information she wanted to share with Colin. She wanted to think about it first.

Friday 27ᵗʰ December 2019 11.00 pm

Returning from another bathroom break, with Anya and

Colin as her guards, Rita's mind was still on Colin's brother-in-law, James Lomax. What was the connection between him and Jai Choudhrie? What had been going on when she had seen them meet? And why had Colin's brother-in-law been killed? What was the connection between what was happening now and the encounters she had witnessed in Exeter and Durham? She was going to have to mull it over some more, and it looked like she would have plenty of time to do so. It felt like she was going to be here for quite a while. Her wrists and ankles, which Anya always tied to the chair now, were getting sore.

Rita had noticed that, once night fell, her captors chose to creep about the room using their phones as torches, rather than put on the main light. Because they kept the beams down, they could probably not be seen from the outside, she thought. How much did the police know about what was happening in the factory? It had been quiet outside for some time now, which was another worry. As if the police had read Rita's mind, before she could be tied to the chair yet again, a woman called Letitia called on Rita's phone. She was one of the negotiators, she told Colin. She asked after their comfort and whether they needed anything. Colin requested blankets and a first aid box. The latter caused some consternation. Was anyone hurt? Did they need medical attention? Letitia was anxious to know. Colin replied in the negative. It was just a precaution, he said.

"Our priority is to get you all out of there safely" Letitia had pushed. "When you're ready, throw the gun out and come out with your hands up. That's all you need to do. No one needs to get hurt."

"Don't tell me what to do!" Colin had snapped, "I'll decide who leaves and when."

Rita had shivered at that. She might need a blanket, she thought.

"You can sleep on the couch, provided you don't try

anything." Jai's voice broke into her thoughts "I'll have to tie your feet though."

* * *

Rita lay curled on the brown sofa by the counter. It wasn't long enough for her to stretch out, and having her feet tied made it doubly uncomfortable. She had a cushion for a pillow. It didn't look very clean, but who was she to complain? Anya had put a couple of the blankets, which the police had provided, over her. Colin was slumped opposite her under another of the blankets. He was sitting on an old leather armchair with bits peeling off it. Jai, she was told, was just outside the door. Anya's whereabouts were not explained.

Would she be able to sleep? Rita wondered. She felt exhausted by what had been going on, but she was tense with anxiety about what was going to happen and her mind was whirring. She was trying to work out the reason for Jai to meet James, Colin's brother-in-law, the man who had been stabbed in the supermarket car park. What did it all mean? The second time she had seen Jai with James was last month, only a couple of weeks before James was killed, when she had made her trip to Durham.

Chapter

7

"Grey towers of Durham! Yet well I love thy mixed and massive piles, Half church of God, half castle 'gainst the Scot, And long to roam these venerable aisles, With records stored of deeds long since forgot."

Sir Walter Scott

Tuesday 5th November 2019 4.00 pm

Going to see her cousins, Rita changed trains at Sheffield. She had with her the blue holdall which Mahir had given her for her birthday, and a matching cross-body bag which she had bought for herself. She listened to music on her phone as the train journeyed northwards, her earphones protecting her from the conversations going on in the carriage around her. The other travellers were a mixture of students, working on their laptops or sleeping heavily, and business travellers, earnestly conducting conversations about targets, pitches, bottom and top lines.

When her aunt Jaina had contacted her on Skype at the weekend, the twins' father, Bandhu, had been in the room, lying on the sofa behind his wife who was perched on one of the arms. His newspaper lay discarded on the floor, Rita could see, as if he had given up trying to read it. He had rubbed his forehead, Rita recalled, as if to say "Can't a man have any peace?" Rita remembered that while the twins were abroad the previous year, before they went to uni, Jaina had been in a stew most of the time and Bandhu had had to cope with all her worry. Now it was still going on. Any hopes he might have had for a quiet life now the young women were at least in the country were not going to be fulfilled, she thought, as her aunt launched into her concerns.

"Shona's had an accident." Jaina had said. her anxiety for her daughter clear from her clipped tone.

"It's nothing serious." Bandhu chipped in. A lot of the drama during the girls' early years, it had to be said, had been generated by what he considered to be his wife's over-concern for their daughters, what he had read was sometimes called 'helicopter parenting'. But, when he had challenged Jaina about this, she had informed him she was a 'tiger mother' and merely looking to give her daughters the best opportunities. Now he had to acknowledge that his offspring were doing pretty well in the drama stakes themselves. The internet did not help. Even as she received the phone message from her daughter, Jaina had sprung to social media, scrolling to find more details about what had happened to Shona. This was something she did several times a day, just to keep an eye on the twins, but on this occasion her search had more urgency.

"She's done something to her ankle. Fell on the wet cobbles. One of the street pastors helped her hobble to a medical station on a bus." her aunt wailed.

"On a bus?" Rita had questioned, wondering what her aunt could mean.

"It's a hospital bus. The University help to fund it. To help the students who are out at night." Jaina explained. "It was 3 in the morning. It saves A&E some work."

"There you are. It was 3 in the morning. I'm not surprised she fell over." Shona's father was less than sympathetic. He had seen some of the Tik Tok videos they made, and what they wore. An accident waiting to happen in his opinion.

"The nurse on the bus said it was probably a sprain." Jaina told Rita, ignoring her husband's intervention.

"She was told to get it X-rayed if it didn't get any better." Jaina added with concern in her voice.

"Humph." Bandhu chimed in from the sofa behind her. From his experience of working in the NHS, this sounded like typical 'wait and see' advice. If things continued, in his view it wouldn't be long before even the nurse on the bus was replaced by Alexa or some similar device that could dispense anodyne advice at no cost to the system.

"And? How is she now?" Rita wanted to know.

"Her ankle is broken" Jaina said, her voice breaking a little. "And it's not easy for her getting up and down those hills, and then there are all those steps to the college."

The twins were both at St Aidan's College, situated at the top of Windmill Hill, with beautiful views over the majestic City of Durham, it was usually approached by a steep flight of steps cut into the hill, Rita had read online. The buildings were modern for their time, having been designed by Sir Basil Spence, who was responsible for Coventry Cathedral, but now they looked a bit dated. The facilities were modern, however, including a gymnasium, music room, shop and bar.

"They must have a disabled access, surely?" Bandhu muttered in the background.

"And Shreya's lost her passport." Jaina made a tutting sound. Rita had noticed how her aunt had a habit of putting her tongue behind her front teeth when she was annoyed.

"Will she need it? In Durham?" Bandhu asked unhelpfully.

"I really should go up there and sort them out myself." Jaina said. "But I thought that might be heavy-handed."

"Really?" Bandhu sat up now, ready, like Canute, to stop this sea of madness creeping up the shore of his home. "They've hardly been gone a month. Let them find their feet." He realised this was an unfortunate expression as soon as he had uttered it.

"Well, our daughters have three good feet between them." he had tried to recover the position, "We don't want it to look like we don't trust them to sort themselves out. After all, they managed to survive abroad on their gap year, didn't they?"

Jaina looked less than impressed at her husband's nonchalance. He seemed to have forgotten that she had micromanaged the twins' trip to India and across to Singapore and Australia, making sure they had relatives or friends they would call in on every few days, and keeping in close contact by phone. Since the girls had been at Durham, however, her calls and text messages had gone unanswered for days, and it had been at least a week since they had Skyped. Jaina found this very unsettling, especially as her daughters seemed to be hitting problems in the first weeks of term.

"So, we wondered if you might go and see them, Rita?" Jaina had asked, pleadingly. "The girls are very fond of you," she tried to flatter her niece, "and they might tell you things they wouldn't tell us."

Well that's the truth, Rita had thought, there was a lot about her cousins that she knew and her aunt didn't.

"Well, OK. Let me think about it" Rita assented reluctantly. She was not sure her cousins would welcome her presence, but if she could get the time off from work there was someone else she could visit while she was in Durham, and that might be rather fun.

Tuesday 5th November 2019 5.00 pm

Darkness was falling as Rita's train slowed on its way into Durham, giving her time to take in the view of the floodlit cathedral and castle from the viaduct on which the train was travelling. In the sky, some early fireworks were piercing the blackness while, down below in gardens, she could see the white trace of sparklers, looking like dancing fairies, probably being wielded by eager youngsters. Bonfire night was still a popular tradition here, she thought, and wondered idly how many people understood the background to the celebrations, the rescuing of Parliament and the kingdom from Catholic insurrectionists. As a child, she had seen the Guy Fawkes story as from another age, and yet now, with ISIS and other groups challenging western society, and carrying out atrocities, it seemed more real.

"Hi, good to see you." Jacob met Rita at the ticket barrier, or 'gate line' as the public announcements called it, at the train station.

"You too" Rita laughed as her curly hair blew in the strong wind and covered her face. She pushed it back and made efforts to fasten it down, placing her bag on the ground in order to do so.

"Amazing view from here!" she said, enthusiastically. The viaduct over which the train had delivered her had given a spectacular panorama of the Norman cathedral and castle situated on what she knew to be a peninsular. The River Wear snaked round the innermost part of the city, providing protection in earlier times and now world class scenery for tourists to enjoy.

"It's pretty impressive, isn't it?" Jacob agreed, picking up her blue holdall. "A world heritage site. That's why it's good for filming this historical series I'm in," he added, bringing the conversation back to himself, a trait with which Rita had become familiar when they had dated. "Although we spend most of the time indoors, on sets specially built to create the interiors." he added.

Rita appraised him as they walked together to his car. He moved more confidently, she thought, and in a more purposeful way than when they had been going out together. It was hard to tell under his jacket, but she sensed that perhaps he was doing a lot of working out. His black dreadlocks were no more. His hair was cropped close to his head now. Overall, it was an improvement, she thought.

Jacob had been pleased when Rita had contacted him to say she was coming up to Durham. He had been missing a friendly face, someone he knew who he could talk to. The other actors were mostly of two kinds. There were the 'old hands', veterans of other tv series, the stage, or films, who were having an extension to their careers by donning historical costume. The other group were young actors, just starting out and anxious to make their mark, always looking over their shoulder at others while trying to catch the eye of talent scouts for new projects. The two groups rarely socialised. The older actors reminisced together or pestered their agents loudly on their phones about Ibsen plays or Becket revivals. They were probably just trying to postpone the inevitable descent into pantomime, Jacob thought.

The younger male actors spent most of their free time in the gym, making sure their bodies were buff for the topless scenes which were becoming an essential part of the series, and were often used in the trailers. Their female counterparts were generally glued to their phones, to the extent that there had to be a 'phone amnesty' before every shoot. They were influencers with Instagram accounts and followers to maintain. Their endorsement of various products yielded rewards far in excess of any available for the average acting job. The involvement of each female actor in the series would seriously boost their earning potential.

Jacob did his fair share of weight training and sit-ups to maintain his six pack, and the director had seemed happy with his topless scene in which, during the 17th century, he had been wrongly accused of stealing apples and whipped for this misdemeanour, the punishment being witnessed by the sensitive young daughter of a farmer, who would become his sweetheart. This was good news, because it meant the will-they-won't-they romance would keep Jacob in the series for another season. He explained all this to Rita as he expertly wove them through the traffic in the rented black Honda Civic the studio provided.

"St Aidan's isn't it?" he checked. He was glad Rita had someone to visit, as it was pretty full-on with running lines, costume fittings and technical rehearsals. The scenes might be short but a lot of work went into them and the director was exacting although, as he told Rita, the AD (assistant director) was helpful and up for a laugh. Once, as a trick on another actor, one of them had hidden in a coffin on the set and risen from the dead half way through the scene. "Everyone corpsed!" he joked. "Oh please!" Rita protested at the feebleness of the pun. There was talk of a BAFTA nomination, he told Rita proudly, although some of the older actors were sceptical, "They always say that" one of them had told Jacob. "It keeps us going."

He listened as Rita spoke on her phone to one of her cousins. "Leave me at the bottom of the hill, I'll go up the steps." she told him.

"OK cool" he replied. It meant he could drop her off and swing by the studio to see if there were any last-minute changes for tomorrow's shoot, when he was going to have a choreographed sword fight with the son of a landowner.

"Let's meet up tomorrow evening, after I've finished work." he suggested. "I can arrange for you and your friends to have a tour of the set, if you're interested." he added.

Tuesday 5th November 2019 6.00pm

Shona and Shreya had looked well to Rita when they met in the entrance hall of the college. They were strikingly attractive, she always forgot that. They had oval shaped faces and long straight black hair, which both wore in plaits that day, emphasising how identical in looks they were. The only way to tell them apart at the moment was Shona's injury. Her leg was encased in a rather fetching black boot shape, and she swung herself around on a couple of crutches. She was quite good at it, considering it had only been on a few days.

As soon as she met up with her cousins, Rita was sure that her aunt Jaina's concerns had been unfounded. The girls were more resourceful than she gave them credit for. They were being well looked after, with en suite rooms cleaned by college cleaners and meals at the college when they wanted to eat there. "Mum insisted we live in for the first year" they told Rita "But we're moving out next year. We're hoping to share a house in Gilesgate. It's only 15 minutes from the town and there's a garden for barbecues!" They seemed to have it all worked out, Rita thought.

"Uni are being very good" Shona told Rita. "The Department email me as much stuff as possible. I just have to get to the tutorials. Luckily, my boyfriend is working in the area and he has a car so he can take me there."

Rita nodded, a sickening fear filling her stomach. Last time she had seen the twins out on a joint date, one of the men had been the brother-in-law of her best friend, Priya. Rita had been to the wedding when Jai married Meera. Now they had two small children. Surely, he wasn't still in the picture? Rita was worried about Jai for another reason, too. She recalled how she had almost bumped into him in Exeter last year and how suspiciously he had behaved. What was he up to?

Chapter

8

"I never weary of great churches. It is my favourite kind of mountain scenery. Mankind was never so happily inspired as when it made a cathedral."

Robert Louis Stevenson

Tuesday 5th November 2019 6.45pm

"Here he is" Shona said excitedly, hobbling on her crutch to the door of her room to open it, having received a message on her phone from the visitor. When it was flung wide there, indeed was Jai, Priya's brother in law, with a silly grin on his face which morphed into a grimace when he saw that Rita was in the room. He even had the nerve still to be wearing the elephant earring that Meera had given him.

"Come in! Come in!" Shona was full of energy, and keen to show off her boyfriend. Jai stepped into the room carefully, as if into a minefield, doing his best to smile at Shona and Shreya while lowering his eyes in Rita's direction, as if by blanking her he could make her disappear.

"This is Rita, our cousin!" Shreya made the introduction as Rita rose from the bed she had been sitting on. She gave Jai a lukewarm handshake, a questioning look creasing her brow.

"Great!" Jai said in a tight voice. "Shall we all go out tonight? I came to see if you fancied the speakeasy." Jai rubbed his hands together as he spoke.

Rita assumed he meant a bar that pretended to be like one during the Prohibition era, rather than one which actually was illegal, At least, she hoped so.

"Oooh yes please!" Shona was thrilled by the idea. "But I

must get changed!" she added, looking down at her denim shorts. "You're all right as you are!" she said to Rita, giving a cursory glance at Rita's black trousers and top. Rita had already left her holdall in the guest room she had been allocated at the College. St Aidan's was named after an Irish monk and missionary who had brought Christianity to Northumbria, she had read in the guide left by the bed in the room. She hadn't brought an extensive wardrobe, so Shona was right, what she was wearing would have to do.

"Jai and I can go and wait in the lobby while you change." Rita suggested. "I saw a vending machine there and I could do with some chocolate." she added.

"Yeh. Good idea!" Shona said, "See you in five!"

"OK" Jai turned on his heels and made for the door, Rita put her blue bag over her head and across the front of her duffel coat, and followed him.

"What do you think you're doing?" Rita hissed at Jai within 10 seconds of Shona closing her door.

"Don't tell Shona," he pleaded, hurrying Rita towards the lobby area "I'd no idea the twins were related to you, Rita." he added, as if this ignorance somehow mitigated his behaviour.

"It's no fun being found out, is it?" Rita said sternly, "And don't tell me it's not been going on for long, I saw you together in a bar in Leicester months ago!" her voice was sharp and accusatory now they were out of Shona's earshot.

"Well, yeh," Jai admitted, "It's been a bit of fun, a bit of light relief, to be honest. Meera and the kids were doing my head in…" he caught sight of the look of disapproval on Rita's face. Rita was remembering the last time she had seen Priya's sister. It had been in the Highcross shopping centre in Leicester. Meera was attempting to steer a baby in its buggy while her older child, Theeran, balanced tearfully on her hip. Not for the first time Rita had fretted about whether she should mention her suspicions about Jai, but she had kept to her resolve not to do so, figuring it was a matter for the family and she should not interfere. Now, having caught Jai in the act, she wondered if she had made the right call.

"I'm going to end it.." Jai was going on. It sounded like he believed it. Jai probably believed a lot of things about himself, Rita thought. Infidelity often went hand in hand with self-delusion she imagined.

"Just don't say anything tonight, please." Jai pleaded. "I'll let your cousin down gently, I promise."

They had reached the lobby by now. Rita scanned the vending machine and selected a bar of dark chocolate, then she took out her bank card and used the contactless payment facility, after which the bar obligingly fell into the metal trough at the bottom of the machine, as if she had won a prize.

Rita reached down to pick it up just as Shona arrived, breathlessly. She had changed her clothes very quickly, and was now in a green velvet top worn over a multi coloured pleated skirt that shimmered when she moved. Over her top she had a black leather-effect biker jacket. Her black booted leg was almost hidden under the long skirt. She looked elegant but practical. Rita approved of her cousin's taste in clothes, if not in men.

As they set off for the speakeasy, Rita realised she had not given Jai an answer. Would she, should she, continue to stay silent?

"Where's Shreya?" she asked, after Shona and her crutches had been manoeuvred into the cab which Jai had ordered. He was travelling in the front, the young women sharing the back seat.

"She's going to join us!" Shona said cheerily, oblivious of the frosty atmosphere between Rita and her boyfriend.

As they reached the innocuous looking door in Hallgarth Street, it gave no clue as to what lay behind it, although the blue light above the door gave the game away for those in the know. Jai rapped on the brass door knocker, and almost instantly the door was swung open by unseen hands, rather as on tv you saw the door of 10 Downing Street open as if by magic. Jai had made a booking; Rita could see why Shona liked going out with him, he was far more considerate with her than he seemed to be with his wife. They were ushered to a booth, where they sat on banquettes, Jai and Shona side by side with Rita opposite. By the time they had ordered their drinks – Jai and Shona went for long island tea while Rita chose a rhubarb cordial - Shreya had arrived. She slid next to Rita.

"Hi, guys!" she greeted them, clearly familiar with Jai as an accompaniment to her sister.

"Hey you!" Jai replied, and they bumped fists in a ritualistic fashion. He really had his feet under the table where her cousins were concerned, Rita thought.

The food was oriental and they tucked into vegetarian hot and sour soup, steamed spinach dumplings, egg rolls, fried rice and vegetable spring rolls, their fingers getting stickier as the meal progressed and the tongues of those drinking alcohol (all but Rita) getting looser.

"There's a regatta on Saturday!" Shona announced, "Can you come?" she asked Jai.

Rita stared across the table. "Sorry, babe" Jai took Shona's sauce covered fingers in his hand, wiped them on a napkin, and kissed them "I have to go away tomorrow. Not sure when I'll be back. I'll be in touch, though." He looked sheepishly up at Rita, his eyes pleading with her not to tell her cousins the truth.

Rita sighed and sat back, reaching for her glass. It would have to do she supposed. Jai excused himself from the table. Rita took a sip of cordial, then asked Shreya to move as she needed to leave the table, too. Rita jumped out of the booth and headed after Jai. She couldn't check in the Gents, but she didn't need to. He had walked past the conveniences to a door at the back, which led onto a patio. It was probably for smokers, Rita thought. A chain of coloured lights decorated the area and there was a picnic table with tell-tale fag ends on the paving stones around it. Rita decided to hang back. Jai was standing under a blue light, so he was bathed in a strange aura when a second man came into view, clearly someone he knew. They bumped fists like batters in cricket, and the man, tall with a beard, handed something to Jai. They exchanged a few words, then Jai turned to come back inside, and Rita dashed to the Ladies.

Rita was first back to their table. Puzzling in her mind what Jai had been doing, she took the opportunity to tell her cousins about Jacob's offer to take them round the set of his television series.

"Oooh, Jacob!" Shona teased.

"Are you two back on then?" Shreya probed.

"Of course not" Rita smiled back, "We're just friends now. Jacob is far too busy with his acting career for anything else. But he would like to see you, if you can make it."

"We'd love to!" Shona said.

"Yeh. Meeting all those actors! What's not to like?" Shreya said.

"What's this? What have I missed?" Jai wanted to know, joining them again. He seemed a little over-excited, Rita thought, and his pupils were dilated. Was Jai taking drugs? Is that what the encounter she had witnessed had been about? Something else she should be reporting to Priya?

Saturday 28th December 2019 4.00 am

"WTF?" Loud music blaring from outside the factory building woke Rita and Colin with a start.

Rita felt she had only been unconscious for a few minutes. It seemed to have taken ages for her to get to sleep, which was not surprising in the circumstances, and then, having nodded off thinking about Durham, the noise had woken her from a dream where she was pounding on the knocker in the northern door of Durham Cathedral, called the Sanctuary knocker. She had learnt that the right of sanctuary was granted by Guthred, King of Northumbria, in the ninth century, and later by King Alfred, and only abolished in 1624. Someone who had committed a 'great offence', like murder in self-defence, or escaping from prison, would be given 37 days of sanctuary during which they could seek reconciliation, or work out how to escape. Monks would have been seated in a chamber above the door to keep watch for sanctuary seekers, and let them in at any time of the day or night. The monks provided food, and the person seeking shelter was given a black robe to wear, with a St Cuthbert's cross sewn on the left shoulder. Rita thought the monks had been wise to time-limit their hospitality, which was at the expense of the Abbot. Look how long Julian Assange had been in the Ecuadorian Embassy!

Rita sat up, rubbing her eyes. Her head felt thick. It wasn't hard to guess why she had had that dream. Escaping to sanctuary looked very attractive, as she woke to face the predicament she was in. Decent food and a change of clothes sounded attractive too. She had no idea what time it was. Outside it looked very dark still. The beat of the music was insistent, some sort of drill music maybe? The sound was unavoidable. Colin reached for Rita's phone, which was on the counter, linked to its charger. "You need to get a new phone" he had told her "It needs charging far too often! The battery's knackered!"

We can't all afford top of the range iPhones bought with ill-gotten gains, Rita had thought, but she had stayed silent, and simply shrugged one shoulder.

"What's going on?" Colin yelled into the phone.

"Sorry, Colin, did we wake you?" Rani, the night negotiator spoke concernedly. It was her turn to be on shift. It was important to keep to the same pattern of voices in order not to alarm the suspects.

"Nothing to worry about. We're having technical trouble with our PA system. Trying to resolve it."

As if in confirmation, there was an ear-splitting squeal, the sound of feedback from a microphone, but magnified several times.

Rita felt her ears recoil and, for a few seconds, she couldn't hear anything clearly at all, like when you've been standing next to the speakers in a club.

"Switch it off or I swear to God.."

No one heard above the cacophony what Colin was promising the Almighty he would do.

Jai and Anya had rushed into the room. When the phone call ended Jai shouted to Colin, "Is it a trick? Can we expect an SAS style entry to the building?"

"I don't know" Colin seemed agitated. "You two check the building. I'll stay here with Rita."

Jai and Colin's wife disappeared to do as instructed. Rita waited, not sure if this was a trap and, if so, who had set it. Had Colin compromised Jai and Anya to save himself? She would not put it past him. Perhaps he was an undercover agent, even an officer himself, sent to infiltrate the criminal network? He certainly knew a lot about police procedures and tactics. How many faces of Colin Shawcross were there?

Rather than look outside to see what was going on, Colin crouched down beside Rita, gun in hand. He was serious and would go down fighting, she concluded, and probably take her with him. He wasn't acting like he was in league with the authorities. Her brain had been doing overtime, probably because she had had so little sleep. Rita felt numb with fear. Were the police coming? They waited. No smoke bombs appeared. There were no dark figures swinging into the room yelling "Get down, Rita!" The noise stopped, abruptly.

"Sorry about that" Rani apologised over the phone when Colin answered it. "Can I make it up to you guys? McDonalds breakfast perhaps?"

Rita realised that, although the sky outside was still dark, it must be the start of another day. Some distance away, she could hear the beat of the blades of a police helicopter. The nearest place for it to land, she mused, would be Abbey Park. At least they were keeping an eye on things.

"Mine's an egg McMuffin" she heard Jai say in the corridor when consulted by Colin, who had told Rani he would call her back. Jai had already reported that no intruders had been found. Colin walked back into the room and called Rani. "That's two egg McMuffins and one sausage and pancakes" Colin ordered as if at a drive-in. It was going to be a long day, Rita thought, as Colin put her phone back on charge on the counter and resumed his place in the armchair.

Saturday 28th December 2019 5.00am

It was a strange brunch that they ate together, sharing three meals between four. Colin was keeping up the fiction that the only people present were himself, Jai and Rita. It felt like very early in the morning to Rita who was trying the remember what time McDonald's opened? Maybe the police had access to a 24 hour one? she mused to herself, irrelevantly, while she nibbled on what McDonalds called a muffin, Anya ate what they called an egg, and the two men tucked into the pancakes. Everyone was irritable from having their sleep disturbed. Perhaps this had been a deliberate police tactic? Rita wondered to herself. Staring with tiredness at the cracked floor, her dream about the lion-like sanctuary knocker was still haunting her. She went back over her visit to Durham in her mind, and tried to recall what she had reported back to her aunt and uncle.

Chapter

9

"I mean that we here are on the wrong side of the tapestry," answered Father Brown. "The things that happen here do not seem to mean anything; they mean something somewhere else."

G K Chesterton

Wednesday 6th November 2019 6.00 pm

The following evening, after a day shopping in Durham and discussing the speakeasy, the three young women took up Jacob's offer to visit the studio where his series was being filmed. Shooting of the film was taking place in an old mining village called Crook, about 10 miles south west of Durham. Jacob sent a car to fetch them. How could they refuse?

The studio was in a former colliery office, a solid brick construction from Victorian times. On the inside, it had been transformed to accommodate various interiors that needed to be filmed, together with all the offices, meeting, relaxation and production rooms associated with filming a series. There was catering on site to suit all palates, as well as dressing rooms, storage for costumes, and the make-up department. They were issued with passes and given an official tour by Petra, a paraplegic researcher on the series, who whizzed skilfully around on a motorised wheelchair, explaining technical issues about lighting – candles were a real bugbear, she said, someone was employed just to light them and blow them out- and camera angles. She seemed to know everyone and to be well-liked. She was greeted cheerfully by all the production staff they met – editors in the cutting room, camera operatives, the costume department, which was extensive, and the fight arrangers, who were just packing up after a long day getting Jacob to have a convincing sword fight with the son of a Lord.

The series, called 'Northern Powerhouse', traced several families through the generations from the end of the English Civil War, following their fortunes as industry, wealth and influence came to their part of England, powered by coal and steam, but also the effective privatisation of land, through enclosure, and consequent social change, starvation and poverty. A frequent theme were the wars of the period. The series focused on the human cost in the sacrifice of mainly young men, and the effect on their families at home.

Petra said Jacob would join them when he had got changed and, in her words, "wiped all the blood from his body". Apparently, although he won the sword fight, he received a bad wound and it was touch and go whether he would survive. Petra told them, in confidence, that the fight would convince Jacob's character to go to Europe in the next season of the series and fight under the Duke of Marlborough.

Listening to Petra, Rita tried to recall the names of some of the battles won by John Churchill, who hailed from Axminster in Devon and became the First Duke of Marlborough, in recognition of his military success. It also helped that his wife, Sarah, was a favourite of Queen Anne. The Battle of Blenheim, in 1704, was the most famous victory, and the palace which was built in his honour, with money voted by Parliament, bore that name. It was in Woodstock, outside Oxford. Rita had visited it early last summer, before she started her internship, when she had spent a few days staying at the house Priya shared with other trainee medics near the John Radcliffe hospital in Oxford.

Less a home, and more a national monument or war memorial, the architect, Vanbrugh, and Lady Marlborough had argued frequently during the construction of the palace. £240,000 was earmarked for the project, although costs overran, as they always do, and the Churchills had to fund the final stages themselves. Rita had learnt that the spectacular setting which Blenheim enjoyed now was created by Capability Brown for the fourth duke over a 10-year period from 1763. He extended the lake begun by Vanbrugh, diverting a river and building a spectacular cascade, and he created two carriage rides into the palace from its imposing entrances.

The victory at Blenheim was highly celebrated because it was the first by a British General on European soil since Agincourt. It had preserved the alliance of Britain, the Netherlands and Austria against the expansionist ambitions of France, led by Louis XIV. Rita remembered from the talk by the palace guide that this was part of the war known as the War of Spanish Succession. It ended with the Treaty of Utrecht which was signed in 1713, consolidating Britain as a great power in Europe.

At Blenheim, Marlborough had fought alongside Prince Eugene of Savoy, another talented general. Marlborough had surprised the French by marching his large army 300 miles to the Danube Valley, making sure the troops were kept supplied on the route, even to the extent of arranging for there to be German cobblers at Heidelberg to replenish the boots of the foot soldiers. The two armies met on opposite sides of the river Nebel. Marlborough, leading from the front, took troops across the river to attack the French at their strongest point, where the infantry endured fierce hand to hand combat. It must have been hell for the ordinary soldiers, Rita thought.

The Duke reported to his wife a 'glorious victory', even though the allies suffered 12,000 casualties. Presumably Jacob's character was not going to be one of them, as he had to get back to England to marry his sweetheart. The Franco-Bavarian army lost 38,000 men. The sumptuous rooms in Blenheim Palace were decorated with enormous tapestries which recorded all of Marlborough's victories, or slaughters, depending on which way you looked at it. It was not only the tapestries which had been created at enormous cost, Rita had reflected.

Winston Churchill, a direct descendant of Marlborough, and born at Blenheim Palace, had naturally praised him highly, placing his tactical skills and diplomacy on a par with Hannibal and Caesar and said that, until the advent of Napoleon, "no commander wielded such widespread power in Europe". It was a pity there was no one to write up the bravery of the soldiers, Rita had thought. She had walked up to the imposing monument built on a rise in the grounds and visible from the Palace. She was disappointed to find it was a victory monument, not a memorial. It had no names etched on it, only the words of the Act of Parliament which honoured Marlborough and afforded the funds for the building.

For a while now, Rita had been taking note of war memorials and other means by which the ordinary men, and later women too, who had lost their lives in battle, could be remembered. Mahir had said it was a harmless hobby, he supposed, and for Rita it was a way of continuing her interest in history, the subject she studied at Warwick University. Every time she went into the centre of Leicester from her family home in Oadby she would pass the tall monument, designed by Sir Edward Lutyens, which graced the entrance to Victoria Park. She had not thought much about it in the past. Now she knew that Lutyens, the designer of the Cenotaph in London, was probably the most famous architect of war memorials. The Arch of Remembrance in Leicester, standing proud and visible from London Road, was the largest example of his work in Britain. She had read that Lutyens was present at its unveiling at 3pm on 4 July 1925 and that a crowd, reported to be 30,000 in number, had turned up to see it. The memorial had no names inscribed on it, so it stood symbolically for all those who suffered or were killed in war and Rita had often found its still presence arching over her a strange comfort as she thought of the fallen on all sides.

There were many kinds of memorials in Leicestershire, she knew. People had put plaques on houses, especially after the First World War, and the Carillon in Loughborough, where Priya lived, the only Municipal Grand Carillon in Britain, commemorated both world wars, as well as the fighting in Korea, Cyprus and the Falklands. It had 47 bells in it, all cast by the local foundry. There were many memorial windows as well, mainly in churches. The East window of Leicester Cathedral was one of them. She wondered how long some of them would survive as memories faded. At least the most recent memorial in Oadby, where she was brought up, was practical. Erected last year to mark a hundred years since the end of the First World War, it was a bench made of black metal with pictures of soldiers and poppies incorporated into the design.

Having seen Jacob, and heard about his role in the series, and the wars which it would cover, as she travelled back to Leicester on the train Rita had found herself dwelling on the waste of young life in causes, many of which were now forgotten. The repatriation ceremonies, when the dead were returned to RAF Brize Norton from Afghanistan and Iraq, had really brought home the cost of war ,and after those conflicts the public's appetite for conflict seemed to have diminished. She thought of something her father had once said, "We used to send young men to war. Now we bang them up in prison where they can be radicalised either by criminal gangs or religious fundamentalists." Now her criminal law experience had led her to hear what prisoners had to say about the conditions inside, she thought there was some truth in this.

On her return to Leicester from her Durham trip, Rita had walked up London Road from the railway station and through Victoria Park to spend some time under the arch and admire the graceful lines of the Lutyens monument. It was a good place to think and she needed thinking time before she met her aunt and uncle at the Diwali celebrations. The day was cool and grey, with drizzle in the air. Rita hoped the damp would not spoil the switch-on later. She had just been pulling the hood of her duffel coat over her head when, out of the corner of her eye, she thought she caught sight Jai in his distinctive yellow padded jacket. Could it be him? What was he doing here? She had been thinking of walking over to him but, before she could do so, he had disappeared. Perhaps she had been mistaken, or perhaps it wasn't him. She seemed to have him on the brain at the moment.

Rita crossed the grass of Victoria Park to reach the main road, from where she could catch a bus to Oadby and drop off her holdall before joining her family on Belgrave Road. She thought back to what Jacob has said about the historical series he was starring in and to the background which Petra had given them on their guided tour. The fact that Jacob was playing a soldier who fought for the Duke of Marlborough and, with luck, would play one of his successors who would fight in India, had made Rita recall a visit she had made with other history students at Warwick University to the Royal Hospital, the home of the Chelsea Pensioners. Here was a place where war and sacrifice would always be remembered.

She had been impressed by the peaceful surroundings in which the veterans lived. The hospital was close to the bustling Kings Road but you would hardly know it. The brainchild of Charles II after he was restored to the throne, the hospital buildings had been designed by Christopher Wren and provided the perfect haven, it seemed to her, with tidy gardens where plants stood to attention in neat rows in between the living quarters. There was a central parade ground where events were often held, they were told.

Rita had peeked into the chapel. There did not seem to be any other religious buildings on the site. Perhaps people of other faiths improvised, she thought. Mosques, Synagogues and Temples would not have featured in Wren's commission she reasoned. The chapel seemed sombre and solemn with rows of polished wooden seats. The dining room looked welcoming, though, with many tables arranged to encourage the residents to socialise. But what had struck Rita most, and what her mind had taken her back to, were the carved wooden panels along each side of the dining room. They commemorated battles and the fallen since the 18th century. Naturally, the ex-soldiers who resided in the hospital (women as well as men these days) would be interested in and take pride in the wars of the past in which their forebears had fought; but to Rita most of the battles recorded spoke of futility and waste.

The commemoration of the dead in the Anglo-Indian wars had caught her eye in particular. A lot was taught and spoken about the expansion and then 'loss' of the British Empire, she thought. But little was spoken about the subjugation of people in the land of her ancestors to which she felt an affinity, although her family had moved from there to Uganda for work and then been displaced in the 1970s. She thought of the supposed Great Indian Rebellion in 1857-58 and how the victor gets to write the history. Before that, there had been many battles between the British East India Company and various Indian States, such as the Mughal and Sikh Empires, and clashes with the Nawabs of Bengal. The boards at the Royal Hospital told only one side of the tale. The creation of Black History Month in October, which had just passed again, was only the beginning for stories of the conquered to be heard. Museums and Galleries, too, were having their eyes opened regarding the exploitation which had so often accompanied the acquisition of their exhibits. We have a long way to go, Rita thought.

Thursday 7ᵗʰ November 2019 7.00 pm

Having left her bag at Elm Drive, Rita took the bus back into Leicester to join her family on the Golden Mile in Belgrave Road. The Diwali procession, the colourful stalls and costumes, took Rita's mind off what she had discovered while in Durham. Their family group hadn't lingered once the procession was over. No one wanted to ride on the Wheel of Light this year. It seemed they were missing the liveliness of the twins, and Jaina and Bandhu in particular were keen to leave to enjoy the meal that awaited them at Padma's house. They walked towards the car park, Rita holding hands with Mahir, who she was glad to see again, Padma and her sister talking conspiratorially as they progressed, Morwenna and Priya, who had joined them for the switch-on and were coming to the meal, keeping in step together, and Bandhu walking with his nephews and discussing football. They were pleased to see how well Leicester City had started the season, riding high in second position in the Premier League. It had been fortunate that after the helicopter accident last year Vichai's son, Topp, as he was known, had taken charge and the appointment of Brendan Rogers as manager had clearly paid off. As they walked along, the fireworks were just starting, flashes lighting up their faces while they strolled in the town centre streets to their cars parked at St George's Way.

As anticipated, Padma had a range of delicious food waiting for them at Rita's family home. Her mother liked to use her culinary skills to bring her family together, knowing that Mohal, her eldest son, would not refuse homemade cooking, Nayan, her youngest child had always been a hungry boy, and Rita, her middle child, enjoyed her food, too. On the way back to the cars, her sister Jaina had once again spoken of her concerns for her twin daughters who were, according to her, having issues in their first term at university. It was obvious that Jaina was anxious for news and Padma was hoping her daughter's report from her recent trip to Durham would reassure her.

Once the meal was on the table, it was Nayan who decided to hold the floor first, making the most of the captive audience to recount gory details from his new role at the police call centre.

"The first thing they teach you on the course," he said, pausing to swallow a smooth and gently spiced mouthful of coconut curry. "Is what the police don't do. So you can direct calls elsewhere. It's quite a list." He spoke enthusiastically about his new job, pausing to tear off a piece of naan bread to soak up the sauce which had pooled around the edge of his plate, like a curry lake.

Padma smiled with pride and satisfaction. It was so good that her youngest son was finding his feet, and to see he had not lost his appetite either.

"Lost property, for example," Nayan resumed. "It's all contracted out now. The police don't touch it."

"Oh" Jaina, Nayan's aunt, sitting between her nephew and Bandhu, her husband, said, surprised.

Bandhu merely grunted and helped himself to more of the curry mixture and lentil daal. He had spent a lifetime working in the health and social care sector and had witnessed the increasing fragmentation of services and proliferation in the bodies providing them, to the detriment of coordination between them. The changes showed no understanding, in his opinion, of the decline in the quality of the service to the patient, or 'service user' as they were supposed to call them now. It sounded as though the police force was going the same way.

"Mmmn" Nayan continued after another forkful, "And

fraud goes to a central call centre, but I'm not sure what they do about it to be honest. I think they just refer you to your bank or whatever. Some of the people I work with took the calls about the helicopter crash, last year."

"It was a terrible event." Jaina agreed. "So unexpected."

The table went silent for a few seconds as they recalled the scenes, twelve months ago, of the players attending a funeral ceremony with Buddhist monks in Thailand. Kasper Schmeichel had summed it up when he said that Vichai had 'given hope to everyone that the impossible was possible, not just to Leicester fans but to fans all over the world in any sport.' Now there was talk of a statue to commemorate him, such was the affection in which he had been held by the whole city.

After a pause, Jaina tried to change the subject to one nearer to her heart.

"But tell me Rita," she said, looking across the table at her niece "How did you find Shreya and Shona?" there was a pleading tone in her voice.

Here we go Rita had thought, and cleared her throat before answering.

Saturday 28th December 2019 5.30am

Sitting in the room in the factory, unsure how long she would be there or how she would get out, Rita tried to remember what edited version she had given to her aunt and uncle.

Thursday 7th November 2019 7.45pm

"Oh, Shona is coping very well with her ankle." she had said. "She seems to be getting good treatment. She can get to tutorials on her crutches and the lecture material is being emailed to her. Hopefully the cast will be off before the Christmas holiday." She paused to scan their faces to see if they were reassured. The jury seemed to be out, judging by their blank faces.

"The University are being very good about it, though." she added.

"And Shreya?" Jaina asked, "How is she getting on?"

Rita swallowed hard. "She's settling in very well. Lots of friends already." She did not mention the new passport or the Sweden trip that Shreya was planning.

"She is very sociable" Bandhu nodded.

"Did I tell you we went on a tour of the set of Northern Powerhouse?" Rita added, hoping it would provide a distraction.

"No!" said Jaina, enviously, the series was one of her favourite programmes. "What was it like? Did you meet any of the actors?"

Rita was saved from lying too much. She spent the next ten minutes describing what Jacob had shown them and the people they had met.

Thursday 7th November 2019 8.00 pm

Finally, Nayan had had enough of Rita's stories and he made a bid to regain the attention of the table. "Fictional dramas are all very well." he said, "But real life is far more interesting."

"Yes, bro" Mohal broke in, gleefully stealing his brother's thunder "Tell them about the head in Leicester Cathedral today!"

Chapter

10

"Where there is no temple there shall be no homes."

TS Eliot

Thursday 7th November 2019 8.00pm

"What's your emergency?" I asked as usual. Nayan told his family, "Imagine my shock when the guy on the other end said he worked at Leicester Cathedral, and they'd just found a carrier bag there with a human head in it!" he announced dramatically as they all stopped eating.

"What?" Bandhu said in case he had not heard correctly.

"Really, Nayan!" Padma started to reprimand him.

Rita, who had been in the process of transferring some curry mixture to her plate dropped the spoon back into the serving bowl with a clatter. She sat back in her chair, the air temporarily leaving her lungs as she absorbed the shock.

"What did you say?" she asked breathlessly.

"I'm telling you, it was a head, from a person, someone had left it in the cathedral. One of the officers there, she found it when she was getting the place ready for a service. Jamie, Detective Chief Inspector Bridge I mean, interviewed her." Nayan garbled out his story which, now he thought about it, wasn't as funny as he had imagined. "I remember all the details. That's our job. Record, retain, reveal all material to the investigating officer." Nayan repeated what he had learnt in training.

"A head? In a bag?" Rita repeated her younger brother's astonishing words.

"Yes, sis," Mohal confirmed. He had heard this story from Nayan earlier that evening and had been hoping to use it in his vlog, except that the police were keen not to have the details revealed while their inquiries continued. They had a head, but where was the rest of the body? And why had the head been left in a public place? The police had released only the details they wanted to, hoping to encourage someone to come forward with more information, so Mohal could not use the gen which Nayan had given him.

"I've been getting information about it for my vlog." he boasted, nevertheless, "I'm sure I could help if the police would let me. You're not the only one who can investigate mysteries." he said to his sister.

"But there was another one recently!" Rita said, which puzzled everyone, "Another head." she said firmly. "It was found in Durham Cathedral. While I was there!"

"What are you talking about, Rita?" Padma's voice had a warning tone in it. "And can we change the subject please?"

"Sure, Mum," Nayan said, "As soon as Rita explains." he added, staring at his sister.

Rita looked anxiously at her mother, then launched into a description of what she knew. "While we were on the set of the Northern Powerhouse," she hesitated as she caught both her brothers rolling their eyes and pretending to yawn, their hands in front of their gaping mouths. Rita had told them all they wanted to know about the drama series, which was of no interest to them, and neither had liked Jacob very much when he had been going out with their sister.

Rita pressed on, "…a local news item came up on Jacob's phone. It said a visitor to the cathedral there had found a bag under one of the pews and it had someone's head in it. The police were appealing for information. That's about it." She shrugged as she finished her story. "I was able to look round the cathedral later that afternoon, once the scene of crimes people had finished looking for clues. It is a beautiful building. Huge and graceful. The first cathedral was built in Durham to house the body of St Cuthbert, which monks brought from Lindisfarne. That was the spot where it rested, so the legend goes. This was in 998. It was re-built by the Normans, alongside the castle, to keep the English under control and the Scots out." she went on "When the shrine to Cuthbert was first built it attracted many pilgrims, even Canute! The Venerable Bede lies at the opposite end of the Cathedral to Cuthbert. All those bodies lying there, and now a head!" Rita finally finished.

"Well, I think we all need some dessert now." Padma changed the subject. "Help me with the dishes, Rita" she commanded.

Thursday 7th November 2019 9.00pm

Three heads, Rita was thinking as she collected up the plates and cutlery. She had thought the Exeter and Durham incidents unrelated until she heard about the head found in Leicester Cathedral, the place where Richard III had been buried with great ceremony not so long ago. Rita had followed his body when it was taken around the city, and to the site of the battle of Bosworth, before its interment. He may have been battered in battle, but at least his whole body had survived, to be buried, lost, and buried again. Three heads but no bodies? Where had the rest of the corpses gone? And why leave the head, the most recognisable part, to be discovered? Presumably the three police forces had identified the victims in each case? It would be interesting to know what they had learnt. Maybe she could ask Nayan to find out.

"Rita!" her mother's voice broke through her thoughts, "Are you bringing those dishes or not?" she asked.

"Yes, Mum!" Rita responded obediently and carried the used crockery, knives and forks to the sink area while Padma took the desserts to the table, so everyone could help themselves and eat them in the more relaxed atmosphere of the conservatory. Rita started to stack the dishwasher.

Thursday 7th November 2019 9.15pm

As she slotted in the plates and cutlery in the way her mother preferred, Rita was thinking about Ganesh, her favourite among the deities. He had been decapitated, which was how he got an elephant's head as a replacement. There were lots of versions of the story, but the one she had learnt as a child was that Shiva had cut it off, either in rage or in battle, and was then advised to take the head of the first living being he found sleeping with its head turned to the north. The first creature that the god came across in such a position was an elephant, and therefore its head was taken to replace Ganesha's. The mixture of animal and human was symbolic. The head of the Lord Ganesha symbolizes the Atman, or the soul, which is considered the ultimate reality of humanity, and his human body symbolizes Maya, the trappings of earthly existence.

Priya broke into Rita's thoughts. She had come to help, and found her friend gazing into space with a spoon in each hand. She started handing the remaining crockery and cutlery to Rita to stack.

"Why would they cut off someone's head and leave it to be found?" Priya asked, puzzled. "It's not that easy to dismember a body you know." she added, thinking of the dissection classes she had attended. "It takes some skill, and you need the right equipment."

"Mmmn" Rita nodded, thinking this was a bizarre subject to be discussing and hoping her mother did not overhear. "As there have been three heads, the incidents must all be connected."

"Wait a minute, three heads? What are you talking about?" Priya was confused.

Rita told her about the head found in Exeter Cathedral.

"Why haven't I heard about this in the news?" Priya

wondered.

"Maybe the police want to keep it quiet for some reason." Rita speculated, "Or it could be a security issue." she said in an excited tone.

"What do you mean?" Priya was puzzled.

"Only that is might be like a spy thing?" Rita suggested, "You know, MI5 and all that. Maybe the heads are Russian spies!"

"You don't really think that." Priya was dismissive. "Three heads.." she stared into the distance, "Makes me think about the giant stone heads outside the Sheldonian theatre in Oxford."

"Oh, yeh." Rita said, closing the dishwasher door and listening to the satisfying whoosh sound as the machine started its wash. It needed to get going. The sweet dishes would need cleaning soon.

"Who are the heads, anyway?" Rita asked, recalling the heads, which she had glimpsed, at one end of Broad Street in Oxford. "The stone heads, who do they represent?"

"Who they are meant to be, no one knows." Priya told her. "And the ones there today are not the originals. There have been three generations. They crumble with pollution, but that means they are a great source for researchers into climate change and the effects of the industrial revolution."

"How long have they been there then?" Rita was always interested when history came into the conversation. "The Sheldonian Theatre was built by Christopher Wren wasn't it? Did he put the heads there too?"

"That's right. It was his first commission, by Gilbert Sheldon, Warden of All Souls College. He wanted a building in which to conduct university business." Priya was glad to be able to tell Rita something. "The iron railings outside the building mark the boundary between the university and the town, town and gown as it were. There are seventeen heads of bearded men, known colloquially as the Emperors' heads, in front of the Sheldonian and what is now the Museum of the History of Science, but was the original home of the Ashmolean Museum. The first set of heads were put up in the 17th century and the second in the 19th. They were replaced again in the 1970s. I don't think Wren had much to do with them. I think I read he left that to someone else."

"Mmmn. Where's the rest of them?" Rita was on a different train of thought, "The bodies belonging to the heads in the Cathedrals I mean."

"They could turn up I s'pose" Priya speculated, starting to move with her friend away from the dishwasher to the conservatory where everyone else was sitting with bowls of the desserts which Padma had prepared. "It's not that simple to dispose of a body, even if you have managed to cut it up."

"Yeh" Rita agreed, thinking of newspaper stories of body parts in suitcases, or buried in gardens. People travelled to parks and woods thinking they could dispose of bodies without being noticed, but their unusual activity often drew attention. Then there was a famous serial killer who had dissolved the bodies in acid, she recalled.

"Heads are significant things. Think of those of traitors which were put on spikes in London. Sometimes heads of enemies would be kept to show they had been defeated" she mused, "While other bodies, or parts of them, were venerated as sacred relics." she said, thinking of Bede and Cuthbert. "Take Edmund for example. He was killed in East Anglia by the Danes in around 870. The legend is he was tied to a tree, shot with arrows and decapitated. His followers wanted to reunite his head with his body and were led by the dead king's head calling 'Here! Here! Here!' but in Latin. His remains were interred at Bury St Edmunds, which became a place of national pilgrimage. He could have been the patron saint of England, you know. Later his relics were moved. I think they are at Arundel Castle now. Hopefully his head and body are together"

"Were you talking about the heads?" Nayan asked, as they joined the others on the wicker sofas, Priya sitting on one side of Mohal and Rita the other. "I'd love to see the shrunken heads, the ones they've got in that museum in Oxford." he said with relish. "They sound gruesome"

"Oh, Nayan!" Priya said, "Trust you! You'll have to visit me and see them in the Pitt Rivers Museum, if you're that interested."

"The heads were treated like that to take away the power of the tribe that was defeated." Rita put in. "I don't think that's why the head was left in the cathedral." she added, although now she came to think of it, maybe that was not so far off the mark. Were the heads a warning?

"Why leave the heads in cathedrals, anyway? Why not Temples or Mosques?" Mohal had posed this question on his vlog.

"Maybe they are easier to access?" Rita offered, "Or perhaps they get more publicity? It is hard to get your head round - oh, sorry!"

"You know why they are called cathedrals?" Mohal asked, ignoring Rita's half joke. He had covered that in his vlog as well.

"Tell us," Priya said helpfully.

"Well, they are large churches, obviously, and a sort of HQ for lots of churches in the area, but the word comes from the Latin for seat, 'cathedra'. It is the seat of the Bishop, the top priest in the area." Mohal explained.

Rita nodded. The Bishop's throne in Exeter was one of the greatest treasures of medieval woodwork in Europe, she had learnt on a visit. It was made in the 14th century using local Devon oak. The one in Durham, which she had seen recently, was built to be the highest anywhere, even higher than the Pope's.

"Well." Nayan put in, more interested in the heads than where they were found, "Jamie thinks..." he continued, referring to DCI Bridge, who Nayan had shadowed for a couple of weeks at Leicestershire Police HQ as part of his criminology studies.

"How come you've spoken to him?" Rita asked, surprised.

"Not spoken, exactly," Nayan was suddenly, and uncharacteristically, reticent. "We chat sometimes online. Nothing he shouldn't divulge, of course. He can't tell me anything about operational matters." Nayan was picking up the vocabulary, Rita noticed.

"What does he think?" Rita got back to the point.

"It's not his case anymore, he's busy with something else, so it's only his opinion." Nayan answered, "But he thinks it's organised crime. That they wanted to send a message."

Chapter

11

"A grove of giant redwood or sequoias should be kept just as we keep a great and beautiful cathedral."

Theodore Roosevelt

Saturday 28th December 2019 11.00 am

Stuck in the disused factory, and eating take-away food, Rita realised she was missing her mother's delicious cuisine, like the meals they always shared at Diwali, drawing together family and friends. That festival involved someone who was captured, Rita's train of thought continued. Sita, believed to be an incarnation of Lakshmi, was married to Lord Rama but was abducted from the forest by the demon Rayana. When Rama defeated the demon he, his brother Lakshman, and Sita returned home. On the second day of Diwali, candles were lit to guide Lakshmi home in the dark, in the hope that she would bestow good fortune for the coming year. There wasn't much sign of good fortune for her, Rita was thinking. Who would come to defeat the demons she was being held by? she wondered. Would her path be lit by candles when they did? It seemed unlikely. She would have to work out her own way of escaping.

Things were getting more relaxed, at least. Colin had agreed that Rita need not be tied up, provided she didn't try anything. So, she was crouched on the brown sofa, while Jai finished the biryani he had ordered, the smell of which would linger all afternoon, she was sure. Rita, anxious for all this to end, turned her thoughts from Lakshmi to Ganesh, her favourite among the gods. Ganesha was said to be Lord over all the atoms and energies that made up the universe, bringing order out of the chaos. Lord Ganesha, the son of Lord Shiva and Goddess Parvati, as god of knowledge and the remover of obstacles, was a handy god for her to think about. What was that phrase she had used in the past?

"Lord Ganesh of curved elephant trunk and huge body, Whose brilliance is equal to billions of suns in intensity, Always removes all obstacles from my endeavours truly..."

She had to believe all her obstacles would be removed and she would be free to roam in her favourite places again. She had once told Mahir that Leicester was the only place she wanted to live. Stuck in this building, Rita decided to list the things she loved about her home town. There was the eclectic mix of people. It was probably the most diverse city in the country. It meant there were food and clothes shops to suit everyone, and carnivals and celebrations for all cultures and religions. It made the city centre a vibrant place. Then there was the history, of course. One of the oldest cities in the country, dating back at least to an Iron Age settlement on the banks of the River Soar. The tribe who lived there were the Corieltauvians, after whom the Romans named the town. In 2013, a Roman cemetery had been found just outside the City walls, Rita recalled. The later name of 'Leicester' came from Old English, Rita knew. The Anglo-Saxon spelling was something like Ligera ceastra referring to the people of the river Soar, called Ligore, and a fort, fortification or town, the term ceastra having been adapted from the Latin castrum.

There were five museums reflecting the City's history and interest in culture- the Guildhall, Jewry Wall, New Walk, Leicester Museum, and Newarke Houses - and Rita struggled to decide which was her favourite. They reflected changes since the Domesday Book, including Simon de Montfort and his struggle against the monarchy in the 13th century, and the building of alms-houses in the 14th century, before the City's role in connection with the War of the Roses, and its final Battle at Bosworth in the 15th century. In Tudor times, there were the connections with Cardinal Wolsey and Lady Jane Grey. During the 17th century there had been the damage the city suffered when it took the Parliamentary side in the English civil war. The city did not really recover until the arrival of the Grand Union Canal in the 1790s and the railway in the 1830s, which enabled the coalfields and industries of the area to develop and find markets. It was because of the success of the textile and hosiery industries that she was sitting in a factory building now.

The Victorian era saw the growth of public institutions and Leicester became a cathedral city in 1927. It was a stopping point for the Jarrow march in 1936. New industries had gradually replaced the old, especially retail, such as the NEXT HQ in Enderby. It was well- placed geographically and had access to the motorways to attract employers, she thought. There was an abundance of shopping opportunities and half a dozen theatres or concert venues to choose from, as well as access to beautiful countryside and parks. And, as she had said to Mahir once, her family was at the centre of her life and they were at the centre of England so why would she want to be anywhere else?

Saturday 28th December 2019 12.00 pm

Rita's thoughts were interrupted. Colin was in the corridor, shouting into his phone again, issuing threats by the sound of it. He was pacing up and down on the brown linoleum, occasionally sighing with frustration, sometimes swearing. The strain was getting to him, Rita thought. That did not augur well for her safety. She cast her eyes around the room, as she had before, but there was no way out that she could see, only the door, and Colin was guarding that.

The more she thought about the things she had heard Colin say to certain clients while at work, the orders he seemed to be giving now to unknown, unseen people, his clear anxiety to protect some sort of unlawful activity he was running, and the stabbing to death of his brother-in-law, James Lomax, the more it felt like he was at the centre of a web of crime, and she had been caught in it... Exactly what criminal activity was being committed, she could not say. But she felt very uneasy about how this might work out.

Chapter

12

"The accounting of the sacrifice is, more than anything else, the attitude toward war memorials in our time."
Friedrich St. Florian

Saturday 28th December 2019 1.00 pm

"So, we have to be prepared to move at any time." DCI Jamie Bridge was finishing the briefing session in the surveillance room. "I don't want anyone caught out having meals or calls of convenience when we get our chance to end this. Make your breaks short and always have cover. Remember, we want everyone out unharmed, if we can, but the priority is the hostage, Rita Patel."

"DCI Bridge." ACC Sue Foster put her head round the door; this was an unexpected and unaccustomed appearance at a briefing.

"Yes, ma'm" he replied, surprised to see her. "Is there something you'd like to add to the briefing?" he rose from leaning on a table and offered her the floor, as it were, although the audience was a small one, consisting of various officers seated in a horse shoe shape on a variety of dining chairs. Among them were the members of the surveillance team, and the leader of the armed response unit, as well as detectives involved in the drug crime investigation.

"Oh, no" Sue Foster looked flustered for a second, and shook her head vigorously. "It's you I want to see. In the kitchen. Now. The rest of you stay here." she ordered.

Jamie Bridge gathered his jacket and followed her; the request had sounded like that of a harassed hostess at a party worrying about the vol-au-vents. What could she want?

In the kitchen/diner the DCI found three officers he had not seen in the building before. They must have entered while the briefing was taking place. They were standing up because all the chairs had been moved next door for the briefing.

"This is Superintendent Turner, Inspector Munro and Constable Rogers, from Professional Standards." Sue Foster made the introductions. With the four of them standing up in the kitchen, it did seem a bit like a party, Jamie Bridge thought for a fleeting moment, before the shock of seeing these officers could sink in.

"DCI Bridge, I need you to give me your phone." the Superintendent, a balding man in his fifties, gave the unexpected order, holding out his hand.

"What? Why?" the questions were out of Jamie Bridge's mouth before he could stop them. "Sir" he added as an afterthought.

"Your phone." the Superintendent insisted, looking very determined.

"OK" the Detective Chief Inspector said, handing over his mobile, which he dug out of his pocket. Superintendent Turner immediately put the phone in an evidence bag before passing it to Inspector Munro, a woman in her thirties, DCI Bridge would guess, with blonde curly hair and large blue framed spectacles. Jamie Bridge thought he might have seen her before, but he couldn't quite place her.

"What's this about?" the DCI asked, not used to this sort of treatment.

"I think you know exactly what it's about." the Superintendent said firmly but mystifyingly, crossing his arms as the two confronted one another in front of the microwave.

"Yes, there is evidence here, boss." the Inspector, who had been jabbing at and scrolling on Jamie Bridge's phone, confirmed to the Superintendent.

"Get it analysed." Superintendent Turner told her, and

the Inspector turned and left the room, taking Jamie's phone with her. Constable Rogers took up position by the door of the kitchen diner, as if the DCI was likely to make a run for it. This operation had clearly been discussed without Jamie Bridge knowing anything about it.

"Jamie," Sue Foster spoke softly, more in sorrow than in anger, it seemed. She was playing good cop, bad cop all by herself, he thought.

"We know what's been going on." she said, looking at his face for a flicker of what? Guilt? Fear? Comprehension? The DCI could not offer any of these.

"I don't understand, ma'am" he said as politely as he could manage. "You'll have to enlighten me." This must be some horrible mistake surely?

"You probably think you've been very clever." Superintendent Turner took over, still talking in riddles.

Jamie Bridge shrugged his shoulders and opened out his arms as if to indicate he had no idea what they were talking about. In case they did not get it, he articulated his response," I have no idea what you're talking about."

"We've revisited what's been going on here." Sue Foster started to explain. The three of them were standing in a small circle now. Who was 'we'? the DCI puzzled to himself, while trying to keep his face blank and his eyes still. He did not want anyone to draw conclusions from his facial expressions or eye movements.

"Right." he said carefully, looking at the tiled floor and waiting to hear more.

"The negotiators were finding the situation, shall we say, odd." the Superintendent elucidated, but not much.

"Odd?" Jamie Bridge repeated "Odd in what way?"

"I won't go into the specifics, if you don't mind." Superintendent Turner said, "We're no longer convinced this is a hostage situation." he went on. Despite himself, Jamie Bridge's mouth opened in astonishment.

"It seems likely there is some complicity going on here." the Superintendent said.

The DCI willed himself to stay still, although he could feel a nerve ticking under his left eye. It was like he had fallen asleep and was having a bad dream.

"Complicity?" he echoed, using the Superintendent's word as a question.

"We realised the suspects have been stalling. Keeping us at bay while they move their stash and their gear out of the building."

"What?" Jamie Bridge put his hands to his head. What could he be talking about? "We can see the building!" he started to protest, pointing to the surveillance room.

The ACC put her hand up as if she were controlling traffic, something he doubted she had ever had to do in real life, such had been the rapidness of her promotion.

"We know there's a back door. We know it leads to the river. We know they've been using barges to clear the place out." she spoke in a sharp tone.

"Well, I don't know that." Jamie Bridge started to object, thinking in his head back to when the factory was first identified by their informant, and who checked out the entrances and exits. It had been one among many operations going on at that time. Superintendent Turner interrupted his train of thought with another devastating statement.

"We know they were tipped off by someone on the force." he went on.

"Surely.." Jamie Bridge began to argue, but the ACC put up her hand again.

"Rita Patel is in the building!" she suddenly added forcefully, banging her hand on the kitchen work top and making some of the mugs jump. "And you're in touch with her brother! Do you think we're idiots?" she snarled.

"What?" Jamie Bridge stepped backwards a few steps, away from the circle formed by his interrogators. Constable

Rogers stepped forward, as if DCI Bridge were about to attempt to escape.

"I'm sorry." Jamie Bridge muttered, signalling with his hand to the Constable that there was no need for alarm. He ran his other hand through his short ginger hair and took a deep breath. "It's just that you must have got the wrong end of the stick." he shook his head. Rita couldn't possibly be involved in this, surely?

The Assistant Chief Constable stood up straighter, scraping her heels on the kitchen floor. "We don't think so, Jamie." she said, "You are suspended while we look into this."

"No, no, this is wrong..." Jamie Bridge tried to object, using his hands in a pleading gesture.

They clearly thought there was a leak, but they couldn't imagine it was him, surely? He had a flashback to a few weeks ago. There had been suspicions then. When that prison officer had been stabbed at Welford Road jail, it had seemed possible that he had been uncovered as an informer, and dealt with, but it could just as well have been random. It was around that time that the DCI had seen Inspector Munro at police HQ, he remembered. She must have been looking at possible suspects among his officers even then.

"Lee will escort you from the building." the Superintendent indicated the Constable by the door. "You know the drill. He needs your ID, pass & badge. Anything you need from your office, you get permission from Inspector Munro, and you are to be accompanied at all times. Pending the outcome of our inquiry, you are suspended." The Superintendent put it on the line for Jamie Bridge.

The DCI's shoulders slumped. There was no point making a scene, he thought. Better that they look into it quickly, realise their mistake, and let him get on with his job.

"All right." he said, moving towards the door, "I'll have to contact my union rep."

"Good idea." Sue Foster said.

Constable Rogers spoke sympathetically as the DCI handed over the items requested. "We'll want you for interview at HQ. Give me your contact number?"

"Leave the building now please." Superintendent Turner said, as if not realising he was kicking the DCI out of a commandeered office in a former warehouse, not a police building. Now it was like being ejected from a party by bouncers, Jamie Bridge thought.

He risked a glance in the direction of Sue Foster. "But I've just done the briefing, ma'am." he heard himself pleading.

"I'll take over for now." she said briskly.

Jamie wished he could go back in to the surveillance room and warn the others. They were in for a difficult time. As he left, the DCI's thoughts turned to Rita. How would she get safely out of the factory building if the police didn't think she was really a hostage?

Chapter

13

Saturday 28th December 2019 3.00 pm

"What is happening to Rita?" Padma wailed.

The dental practice she ran was closed until the new year, even for emergencies. The notice on door said 'Closed for personal reasons. Apologies for any inconvenience'. Even if it had not been, neither she nor anyone else at the practice could have concentrated once the police, a young looking black female Sergeant, and an Asian Constable in a uniform that looked too big for him, had called at 10 Elm Drive that morning with the news that Padma's daughter was not, as she had thought, at the flat she shared with Morwenna Maitland, but was in a disused factory near Abbey Park, apparently being kept hostage.

"Try to drink something." Mahir Sharma was as worried as Padma. He was also a little afraid of Padma's tears and he thought, if they were kept occupied, she might be less inclined to have an emotional outburst. He had miscalculated. It was amazing how shrill the sound of a worried mother's voice could be as Padma put down her cup and her face crumpled under the weight of her fear.

Saturday 28th December 2019 6.00 pm

Back in his penthouse apartment that evening, after a long bike ride out to Uppingham and back, to get rid of some of his nervous energy, DCI Jamie Bridge showered and changed into track suit bottoms and a Leicester Tigers rugby top. The time had dragged along that day and he felt impatient, as well as worried about his interview tomorrow with Professional Standards, what was happening to his team and, above all, the plight of Rita. He needed to return to action as soon as possible or he would explode with frustration. He poured himself a whisky, swilling it round in the glass before settling in his Eames inspired lounge chair, placing the whisky next to his notebook on the nearby smoked glass table.

Constable Rogers had called late than afternoon. His interview was set for tomorrow morning. Another day of cooling his heels beckoned. They were taking their time, he thought. They must know he wasn't the leak, if there was one at all. He sighed. All this was wasting time, while the criminals made fools of the police and kept Rita for another night.

He had decided to tease away at the strange appearance of the heads, meanwhile. Perhaps he could make headway with that (ha ha!). The head found in Leicester had in fact been identified. The breakthrough came when they realised, he (it was a he, the pathologist was confident) had distinctive bridgework in his mouth. An appeal had gone out to local dentists in the hope that the man was from the area. If that had drawn a blank, they would have cast the net wider. But there was no need.

It was that chap from the surgery that Rita's mother ran who had contacted the station. Jamie Bridge could not remember his name. He had met him, though, in the past, on another case. He seemed nice enough and Nayan confirmed he was reliable. What was it that Nayan had told him about heads being found in cathedrals elsewhere? He could, of course, have consulted Rita's younger brother, but at the last minute his offer to do a shift at the call centre had been taken up, and taking private calls was frowned on. He didn't want to get Nayan into trouble.

Rita's younger brother had told Jamie Bridge about the family meal, the one his mother arranged in November after they had been to see the switch-on for Diwali. The DCI had been in Nottingham that day, chasing up a lead on a stabbing incident. He remembered seeing the fireworks light up the sky as he returned to Leicester. It was quite a spectacle. Rita had said something at that meal. What was it? Oh yes, Nayan said she had been in Durham to see some family members who were students there. They couldn't be nieces, so they must be cousins, perhaps? It was Nayan who had taken the call about the head in Leicester Cathedral and he had talked about it at the meal, even though he knew he shouldn't have, he had admitted sheepishly to Jamie. He could hear Nayan's indignation now.

"There I was, everyone listening to me, wanting to hear all about the head, and Rita says…" he had paused for dramatic effect, "She butts in and says, casually, 'Oh yeh, there was a head left in Durham Cathedral, too. It was on the news. While I was staying there.' And then everyone turns their attention to her! I ask you!"

Jamie Bridge wrote on his pad 'What did Rita know about the head found in Durham?' What did his police force know, come to that? He had not heard of any other heads being found, but each force tended to operate separately, as if crime respected borders. It was a weird coincidence if the incidents were not the work of the same organisation. Had there been others? DCI Bridge picked up his iPad and consulted Inspector Google with one hand, his whisky glass in the other. What he found made him almost drop the glass. He put it back on the table. He reached for his phone, suspension or not he would have to make a call. He found the number for a Sergeant he knew in the Devon and Cornwall force.

Chapter

14

"Ruins are the cathedrals of time."

Marty Rubin

Sunday 29th December 2019 11.00 am

DCI Jamie Bridge had been questioned at length, with his union representative present, even though it was a Sunday. Time was of the essence, Sue Foster had agreed when she finally took his call. He needed to be cleared of any wrongdoing so he could get back to freeing Rita. He had tried to impress on his interrogators - Superintendent Turner and Inspector Munro - that they were wasting time. If there was a corrupt officer who had been tipping off the criminals in the factory, it was not him. They needed to forget about him and focus on who it actually might be. They hadn't seemed to listen but he hoped they had, in fact, taken note.

He gathered from their questions that, while the police were watching the front of the building, the factory was being emptied from the back, where there was access to the River Soar. Once boats had been loaded with drugs, and the equipment to process them, they could be taken either up to Leicester Marina, and moved on from there, or, more likely, down to Aylestone where the river joined the Grand Union Canal on its southward journey. Police officers had swarmed the area around the Marina, to the astonishment of the owners with craft moored there, and drawn a blank. No one had seen additional activity or craft being unloaded in a hurry. Looking at the idyllic scene, with boats nestling in the quiet Marina in the natural surroundings of Watermead Park, the officers sent to check it out had concluded early on that this was an unlikely place for organised crime. "They must have gone south." they reported.

"Who had initially checked out the factory?" the Superintendent wanted to know. "Why hadn't they reported about the river access? Why had the suspects been allowed to clear out the factory under their very noses?"

Jamie Bridge could only tell them so much. As the logs would show, the officers who checked out the factory, when it had been pinpointed by their informer, were DCs Yousef Mohamed and Trissey Adams. They had told him the back of the building was in a poor state of repair and obscured by tall grasses and other plants. There was no exit from the back he had been told.

"You must have had plans of the building?" the Inspector pressed.

"Well, we asked." Jamie Bridge confirmed. "The council planning department had nothing and the fire brigade came up blank too. The building was too old for computer records and any paper ones were probably lost during the war, the Second World War I mean. A lot of records went missing in the bombing of the city. We only had the description of our informer to go on, and that was pretty sketchy."

"Nayan Patel." the questioners changed tack. "Why were you in such constant contact with him? Your email account and phone log show frequent calls and messages, well before his sister went into the building."

"Nayan did some work experience with me, that's all." Jamie Bridge explained," He's doing a Criminology PhD at Leicester University. It's about the causes of crime. He's very keen. He might even join the force when his studies are finished. We never exchanged any information on operational matters." he said insistently, starting to feel impatient at these intrusions while the real officer at fault remained free.

"And why did his sister go into the building?" the Inspector asked.

"I really don't know!" the DCI protested. "I was as astonished as you were. Now I am worried for her safety." he added honestly, "From past experience, she acts first and thinks later. I think she's walked into a situation she wasn't expecting."

"She went in after Han Solo?" Superintendent Turner queried. He was in his shirt sleeves, his jacket on the back of his chair. Jamie Bridge wasn't sure if it was to intimidate him, or if the Superintendent was naturally warm blooded. The DCI, by contrast, had carefully selected a navy suit and tie, and kept his jacket on.

"Yes. You can see from the footage." Jamie Bridge said tersely.

"They weren't together?" Inspector Turner pressed.

"I don't think so, no." the DCI shook his head. "From what we could see, Han Solo went through the door first. Rita Patel walked in a good thirty seconds later."

"Which brings us back to the question, why is she there? Is she in league with Chewbacca and Han Solo?" the Inspector, who had taken off her glasses, shook her head. Her fair hair was tamed today by a scarf tied on the top of her head. It gave her the appearance of one of those land army women on Second World War posters.

"I'm sure she's not." the DCI felt he was having to defend Rita as well as himself.

"But both the suspects are known to her?" the Inspector would not let this go.

"As we now know, yes." Jamie Bridge conceded. "Chewbacca works at the legal firm where Rita is employed and Han Solo, we discovered, is the brother-in-law of a friend of Rita's, but that doesn't mean she's involved." he protested.

"Really? Are you sure?" the Superintendent was not convinced. "If it was anyone else would you be arguing like this?"

"What do you mean?" the DCI asked, noticing his union

rep raise her eyebrows in warning. This was dangerous territory, he knew, but he had to get Professional Standards to focus elsewhere for their mole.

"You've had dealings with this young woman before, you are very pally with her brother…perhaps she's been playing you." the Inspector suggested.

"No!" Jamie Bridge, pushing his body away from the table in protest, was getting irate now, despite his union representative shaking her head vigorously.

Another officer from Professional Standards entered the room and spoke in the ear of the Superintendent, who nodded, rose and, surprisingly, said, "OK Detective Chief Inspector, we can wrap it up there." adding as he put on his jacket, "We'll be in touch."

"But when can I get back to my duties?" Jamie Bridge queried as they all rose to leave the room.

"We'll be in touch." was all the Superintendent would say. The union rep shrugged her shoulders as if to indicate 'what can you do?'

Sunday 29ᵗʰ December 2019 11.00 am

"Why does this have to happen to Rita now?" Padma moaned, raising her hands in despair. "Just before the wedding. Do you think she's going to be all right?" she turned to Mahir ,who was giving her a lift to the office of the wedding planner. "You must be so worried about her" she added, seeing his concerned expression.

"Of course I am" Mahir admitted, swallowing hard. "But there's nothing we can do. We have to trust the police. I am sure it will all be over soon."

Padma pursed her lips. She did not look convinced. At least she need not worry about the business. The Manor Gardens Dental Surgery, on Uppingham Road, was now closed until the new year, as planned. One reason the wedding had been planned for New Year's Eve was that everyone would be able to get away for it. That had been the intention anyway.

"We need Rita here for the wedding practice!" the wedding planner had complained on the Wedding WhatsApp Group earlier that day. "Her absence has put my schedule right out!"

Sunday 29th December 2019 11.30am

All the women involved in the ceremony (minus Rita) were sitting together on a large, pale green, L-shaped sofa in the planner's office. They were looking at the planner's schedule on her iPad screen, which they passed among them. Glasses of fruit juice had been supplied, together with a platter of fruit. Behind the pale green screen, all their outfits were arranged, to make sure no one was lacking anything. The hanger containing Rita's clothes, with her shoes and jewellery in a box beneath it, had looked particularly poignant.

"I just hope she's OK." said Priya, pulling her fingers through her brown black hair extensions, a recently fitted addition.

"Steady" the wedding planner ('Susie Day for Your Day') admonished her "You'll pull them out before the big day and we don't want that do we?" Really, this was one of the most difficult situations she had ever been involved with, she thought. Would the siege end in time for the wedding? No wonder everyone was on their nerve ends.

"Shall we go through the flowers and the wedding favours again?" she said brightly.

Chapter

15

"Cathedrals, luxury liners laden with souls, Holding to the east their hulls of stone."

W. H. Auden

Sunday 29th December 2019 1.30 pm

Mahir picked up Padma from Susie Day's office, and drove her to the café where they had arranged to have lunch with Nayan. Neither of them felt like eating, but Mahir hoped that being with other people might stem Padma's tears and, for once, Padma was not interested in cooking. Mahir wondered how he would get through the next few hours himself. The time without Rita had dragged and each hour she was missing increased his anxiety for her. All his reassuring statements to his boss and future mother- in- law disguised his real feelings on the subject of Rita's capture. He was tormented with thoughts that she might be frightened, or hurt, or both. The police would tell them nothing about who was holding her, or why, beyond saying it was part of a larger investigation and they had the situation under control. It sounded like platitudes to him.

Rita was impetuous, he knew, and he loved her for it. She was resourceful, too, but he sometimes wished she did not need to be so independent. Like the time she had taken herself off to Devon to help her friend. She had needed to make herself useful while she waited for her internship, he understood that, but his heart had sunk when he looked at a map and saw how far away Totnes was. He had the dental practice to help to run, so he could not take much time off to see her, and there was his family to think of. Since his wife had been tragically killed, he was an important figure in the lives of Aashi and Sadhil, although he did have his wife's mother to help with the childcare. Soon he would have two mothers-in-law; he managed to smile to himself.

What could Rita have been up to? How did she get to be inside that factory? He could not work it out. The last time they had spoken she said she was going into town to look at a war memorial. War monuments had become a thing of hers, he knew. When she had been in Totnes, she had been thrilled to find a fine example in the grounds of a church. "It's Grade 2 listed!" she had told him excitedly on the phone." It's a granite memorial with a cross designed by Sir Reginald Blomfield. He was one of the principal architects commissioned by the War Graves Commission, like Sir Edwin Lutyens. It commemorates 103 men from Totnes who died in the 1914-18 war, and then they added the names of 38 more who died in the Second World War. It was unveiled in 1921 and paid for by public subscription; it cost £277." There were worse hobbies, he had thought, and looking at war memorials was, sadly, something you could do in almost every town and city in the country. Surely that had not got Rita into any trouble?

He thought back to a recent telephone conversation with her.

Mahir had been at home, looking at a series of images on a police officer's iPad. When Rita had called to ask what he was doing, he had taken great delight in saying, "Helping the police with their inquiries." Rita had laughed. They had discussed beforehand the fact that he might be able to help. They had seen the appeal by the police for dentists who might be able to identify the person whose head had been left in Leicester Cathedral. Details were emailed to all surgeries. Dr Sharma had picked up the email at home, and it put him in mind of a particular patient. "Of course, I might be wrong." he had told the call handler.

Mahir had tried to sound casual on the phone with Rita, but the task confronting him was more unpleasant than he had thought. He was used to patients who were alive. Even though he was a dentist with years of medical training behind him, he found the pictures he was being shown by the police shocking. The head had been hacked off rather crudely, he saw, and the man, it was clearly a man, had been subjected to some brutal treatment beforehand. The police officer, DC James, had told Mahir he could take a break or look away. They did not want to give him PTSD, after all. He tried to swallow, but his mouth was dry. He reached for the glass of water in front of him without taking his eyes from the screen until he was sure. Finally, he was satisfied. The images had shown the object from all sides. Some were blown up parts of the image, some showed the whole thing.

"Yes," he said slowly, "That's the head of my patient."

Steven Coleman, a man in his late twenties, had shuffled reluctantly into the surgery about a year ago, he recalled. For a graduate in Bio-medical sciences, it was surprising how scared he was of visiting the dentist. Mahir had to put him at his ease. That was how he discovered he was a man with a chip on his shoulder – "You missed your vocation," Samira, the dental nurse, said afterwards, "have you thought of psychiatry?" Mahir had thought it was worth taking the time to settle the patient. It made treatment easier in the long run. Steven Coleman, he had learnt, worked in a research lab, but regretted not having stayed on at uni to do a PhD. "The PhDs get all the glory while we do all the work" he had grumbled. "We are treated worse than the lab rats." Once Mahir looked in his mouth, it was apparent he hadn't been looking after his teeth very well and, not being one to judge, from the state of his teeth and gums and general demeanour, Mahir wondered if he took drugs. The toothache had been caused by an abscess, for which Mahir prescribed antibiotics, before he could examine his teeth more closely. "Make an appointment for a week's time." Mahir had told him, printing out the prescription and a sheet with his diagnosis and treatment plan.

"Might be a bit tricky." Steven Coleman had said. "I'm on nights for the next fortnight."

Mahir, who had not been aware that research labs worked overnight, had said surely his employer would understand? to which Mr Coleman had snorted "Yeh, right. I work two jobs to make ends meet, you see." Mahir had nodded, wondering how much the Inland Revenue knew about the two jobs. If Steven was a drug user, perhaps he needed extra income to feed his habit? Mahir had speculated. Steven Coleman had returned, eventually, and Mahir had given him some root canal work and fitted a large metal crown in his lower left molar, as well as a couple of other fillings, and recommended he see the hygienist. He hadn't seen the patient since.

Mahir had been fairly sure it was Steven Coleman when he saw the dental information on the police email. Now he had seen the image of the severed head, he was certain. He was shown the head first of all front on, then the left side, the back and then the right profile. To assist further, the pathologists had obligingly opened the head's mouth and photographed the teeth. The appearance of the left molar clinched it for Mahir, although he really had had little doubt.

Sunday 29th December 2019 1.30 pm

Arriving at the café first, Nayan ordered a snack and spoke to Mohal on his phone while he ate it. Rita's brothers were doing what they could. Mohal was vlogging about the siege, although there was precious little information to discuss. Various people in the area had photos of the scene which he put on line. The pictures were inevitably taken from a distance, as the police had put a cordon around the immediate vicinity of the stand-off. But curious onlookers had powerful phones these days and there were good vantage points from the higher floors of nearby buildings. Not that it was possible to see much from the photos. The red brick art deco façade of the disused factory gave nothing away. The peeling double doors at the front remained closed. Some of the watchers had said they thought they could see movement at one of the windows, but even when enhanced there was nothing definite to see on the pictures. There might be a shadowy figure there, but discerning it was like trying to trace the Loch Ness monster in a pool of ripples and reflections. The area immediately in front of the factory was deserted and, further back, there were police vans.

Any police officers were hard to discern, apart from those in uniform who were enforcing the cordon to prevent anyone getting close. Presumably the operation was being run from inside a vehicle. There must be a negotiating team, Mohal had told his followers, but there was no one shouting at the hostage takers through a megaphone like you saw in TV dramas. Nayan, with a few weeks of work experience at the police station under his belt, had told his brother that in all likelihood communications would be conducted by phone and that the time it was taking to get the matter resolved should not be of concern. He said the aim was to keep the perpetrators calm and make things as comfortable for everyone as possible; the police try to keep the temperature down, Mohal confidently relayed to his followers.

Sunday 29th December 2019 1.45pm

When Padma and Mahir arrived, Nayan had an empty plate in front of him and had ended his call with Mohal.

"Any news?" his mother asked him anxiously. Nayan shook his head regretfully. Nayan had, the family knew, been in touch with DCI Bridge from the very start. He had, after all, been talking to Rita when she had gone into the factory building and he had heard a shot. So, thanks to Nayan and Mohal, the outside world also knew the suspects were armed, but, even if this had been a secret to begin with, that particular cat was let out of the bag when the armed response team arrived. It was their practice on this occasion not to hide their presence but to ostentatiously take up positions on rooftops opposite the factory as if to warn the hostage takers not to take any drastic action or there would be consequences.

Nayan had offered to do a shift at the police call centre while the siege continued, but his shift leader had said he should take time off during this stressful period. He had uni work he could catch up with and had brought his laptop to the café, fully intending to work before he got caught up with the call to his brother. Somehow, despite his good intentions, it was proving hard to concentrate on the research he needed to do. As well as the fate of his sister, something else was bothering him. Without giving a reason, DCI Bridge had stopped replying to his calls and messages. Nayan would have gone round to his flat to see what was going on, but Padma needed him at home. She disliked letting another child out of her sight until Rita was restored to them, assuming she would be, he thought despondently. Suddenly his phone vibrated. 'Come and see me' the message said. Jamie Bridge had also given the address where he would be.

"Er, I have to go somewhere..." Nayan began, picking up his laptop. "Not for long.." he added, seeing the look of concern on his mother's face. "And I might be able to find out a bit more about what's happening to Rita." he added to get parental approval.

"OK" Padma said hoarsely, dabbing her eyes with a tissue.

"I will take care of your mother." Mahir said solemnly. "I will make sure she is not alone" he reassured Nayan who nodded his thanks and walked to the door of the café.

"She will be all right." he reassured his mother as he left.

"What are you having?" Jamie Bridge asked Nayan Patel as he exchanged the café where his mother and Dr Sharma were attempting to eat something for Dev's, a food shop and café a few hundred metres from the sealed-off factory site where Rita was being held. Dev's was a useful source of refreshment for the officers on duty there. This unexpected event was a boon for business. Nayan had caught a bus from the city centre and walked the rest of the way. He was hoping Jamie Bridge might have a car and be able to give him a lift home, otherwise he would be late for dinner. Now he saw the extent of the food available at Dev's, he saw this was not going to be such a problem.

Nayan ordered a curry and rice dish plus a couple of samosas, and the two of them shared the food while they talked.

"Why did you tell me to switch off my phone?" Nayan asked as they gathered cutlery, napkins and glasses of water in preparation for the meal.

DCI Bridge checked to see who was in the deli before he replied.

"Look, I've been suspended."

"What?" Nayan shouted in surprise.

"Sssh! Keep your voice down." Jamie Bridge asked, "Let's not draw attention to ourselves. I probably shouldn't be talking to you at all and for God's sake don't breathe a word of this to your vlogging brother."

"Why not?" Nayan was whispering now, which drew the attention of Asha, Dev's brother, who was at the counter.

"There's a leak." Jamie Bridge explained, adding, urgently, "But you can't tell Mohal. If this gets out, I'll never get reinstated."

"What do you mean?" Nayan spoke urgently now the seriousness of what was happening was starting to dawn on him.

"They think it's me. Because of our calls." the DCI went on. "I can prove it's not, but they have to go through the motions."

Nayan's mouth was still open in astonishment when Asha came to put the food down on the table. The two men picked up the cutlery and dived into the curry, pausing to take bites from the samosas and speaking to each other with mouthfuls of food.

"How long will it take for them to be satisfied it's not you?" Nayan wanted to know.

"Hard to say. Hopefully a couple of days." Jamie Bridge told him.

"A couple of days!" Nayan raised his voice again.

"I know. I know" the DCI shook his head regretfully. "That's why I'm sitting in here." He explained, "I can't be within the cordon and I have to go to the station to answer any questions they have, but they can't stop me sitting in a public café." then he lowered his own voice to a whisper, "Trissey comes in here for food for the troops. I can keep up to date with progress by talking to her." Nayan let out a sigh. He could see that Jamie Bridge was making the best of a difficult situation. What else could he do?

Sunday 29th December 2019 3.00 pm

"She will be OK, won't she?" Padma's voice was trembling as she put her cup back on its saucer. Her hand was shaking and the cup rattled on its descent.

"Of course, this is Rita we are talking about, she's been in scrapes before, hasn't she?" Mahir tried to reassure, looking down at his own cup, which was his second drink that lunchtime. Neither of them could face eating very much, so the café was not making much money out of them that day.

Padma's daughter was a risk taker, he knew that, and her

love of solving mysteries had got her into trouble in the past. He was keeping his fingers crossed that she hadn't gone too far this time. As he drove Padma home, Mahir thought back to the evening of the hen party, which he had thought would be the last time he had to see Rita in danger. How wrong he had been.

Chapter

16

"I don't know what London's coming to — the higher the buildings the lower the morals."

Noel Coward

Sunday 29th December 2019 3.00 pm

In the factory, as the hours dragged by, Rita was thinking about the hen night too. She needed something to take her mind off this situation and to stop her from speculating about what might be going to happen. The hen party had been arranged for a few months before the date of the wedding. This was because of Priya's rotations and shifts now she was well into the clinical part of her studies. "I just can't get away when I want to," she had told the wedding planner. "It has to fit in with my hospital work." It also meant that Rita's twin cousins could join in, before they started their studies at Durham University. Rita hadn't minded doing it early. Her work in the Criminal Department was proving tricky, so it provided a welcome distraction. The party had gone well, until… but she didn't want to think about that part.

Friday 20th September 2019 9.00 pm

"Tell us how he proposed!" the group of six young women were sitting in Nawaaz, a restaurant on London Road famed for its Indian food. They had started out at Exquisite, a nail bar in Oadby, and gone from there for drinks (champagne or mocktails) in Henrys Champagne Bar in Pocklington Walk. They had put themselves in the hands of Ayeesha, Priya's hyperactive friend, which with hindsight might have been a mistake, although it had gone pretty smoothly so far.

No one wanted a lot to eat. They all had dresses to fit into, even if the wedding was a few weeks away. They asked the rather good-looking waiter for poppadoms and some vegetable dishes.

"Oooh. What a well fit dude!" Shona said when the waiter had gone. Rita took this to be a good sign. Perhaps she was getting over Jai?

"Hands off, I saw him first!" Shreya said. "A real dreamboat!"

"Yes, you did call him over, to be fair." her twin conceded. "I'll have to bag another one!" she giggled.

"Not bringing a plus one to the wedding?" Priya asked.

"Too right, we are!" Rita's cousins had replied together. "We both have boyfriends who will do for now." Shreya said rather casually, "But they're not The One" she added. "How do you find the right one these days?"

"I'm not sure we should be discussing that tonight!" Priya laughed.

"No, but seriously." Shreya wanted to discuss the subject. "You and Rita are ok, but what about us?" she added, "In the past our parents would have just arranged a match for us."

"Yuk!" Shona said, "I really wouldn't fancy that. Imagine marrying someone you did not know."

"It's surprising how often it worked." Rita put in. "I guess the families would do their research. And everyone lived in small communities where they knew everyone else."

"But now that's not the case." Shona sighed. "You're all right." She addressed Morwenna who, to the girls' knowledge, was never short of a good-looking boyfriend. "Well I s'pose there's no family pressure." Morwenna conceded, "But I know what you mean about finding the right one. I always thought I would have found someone to settle down with by the time I was 25 but time is running out and there's no sign!"

"What about Adam?" Shreya asked about Morwenna's current boyfriend.

"Oh, he's fine for now" Morwenna did not sound enthusiastic.

The others started to protest, telling her how good looking he was with his Italian looks and long eyelashes.

"Oh, I know!" she conceded, all her boyfriends had been good looking, it was a given. "He doesn't want to settle down any more than I do. We have fun together, and he'll look great in the wedding photos."

Shona and Shreya nodded to show they agreed with that.

"What about dating agencies?" Morwenna asked the twins, "Have you tried Tindr?"

Shona laughed. "We wouldn't get away with using a site like that!" she said, "Our parents would be horrified. They expect us to use Hinge so we will meet 'suitable boys'. But the trouble is, the pool is limited."

"What's worse" Shreya added, "Is that the site discriminates against the untouchables. It perpetuates the caste system."

"Oh" Morwenna was taken aback and tried to absorb this information, which she had never thought of before, as the fit waiter arrived with the food they had ordered.

The young women started to scoop portions of the savoury dishes onto their plates, using the large white napkins to protect the pink T-shirts which they wore to identify themselves as part of the same hen party. As agreed, they wore shalwar kameez trousers and pink shoes.

It was at that point that Morwenna had changed the subject by asking about the proposal, and the conversation had moved on from dating agencies.

Friday 20th September 2019 11.30pm

The hen party had conga'd in an uncertain pattern around the intersection of London Road with Regent Street. Various menfolk had been designated to pick them up in the railway station car park, which was not far away.

"You are not getting in my car if you are too drunk." Mohal had said. "Don't even think about it." Bandhu had told his daughters, thinking of the upholstery in his Dascia Duster.

They weren't drunk on alcohol, just happiness and the freedom to enjoy and express themselves. They had toasted the forthcoming wedding in apple juice. The conga line moved a little way down Regent Street like a staggering pink caterpillar. As usual, Morwenna carried off the hen party look the best. She had made it look fashionable with a wide pink plastic belt at her waist and her pink shoes which were trendy trainers.

"Keep up! Keep up!" Ayeesha was yelling from the front. She was aiming for New Walk which was a pedestrianised area, a promenade with no vehicles allowed, created in 1785 and reputedly on the site of a Roman road. The walkway linked Victoria Park to the heart of town. It was a favourite route of Rita's, Ayeesha knew, and it would be easier to conga down there she thought. Suddenly, she stopped and the conga line tripped over itself as it came to a halt.

"Be careful!" Shona said, who, never very steady in her shoes, which were pink platforms, had been at the back.

"Smoke!" Ayeesha shouted to those behind her, most of whom were sprawled on the pavement. Rita looked down at Morwenna, who was next to her and sitting at the kerb, with a puzzled expression.

"I don't want to smoke." Shreya said in a tired voice, confused.

"No" Ayeesha insisted. "That's not what I meant. I can smell smoke."

Rita sniffed the air. Ayeesha was right. Where was it coming from? There were hotels and guest houses in the area. Maybe there was a kitchen fire? No, she could see flames now. They were coming from a house across the road, opposite the shop near which they had stopped so abruptly.

"It's there!" she shouted, "Call the fire brigade!" she yelled, thinking it would not take them long to come, the fire station was only down the road. Then she ran over towards the fire, Priya chasing after her, advising her to be careful, but that was a waste of breath where Rita was concerned.

Chapter

17

"In short, the anomaly of war is that the best men get themselves killed while crafty men find their chance to govern in a manner contrary to justice."

Emile Chartier

Saturday 21st September 2019 12.00 am

Mohal, Adam, Bandhu and Mahir were waiting by their cars at Leicester station car park as agreed. Strictly speaking, it was 20 minutes waiting time only, but it was so late at night (or early in the morning, depending on which way you thought about it) that few trains were stopping and no one seemed to mind. Mahir had brought Nayan with him, but, rather than stand outside with the others, he had stayed inside Mahir's car, talking to someone on his phone.

"The girls should have been here half an hour ago!" Mahir fretted, "No more news from Priya?" he asked Mohal.

"No." Rita's brother shook his head, wondering what to do next. "After Rita sent that last message that they would be later than they thought, there's been nothing."

"Morwenna's not replying either." Adam confirmed. "It's like the girls have gone off the grid."

"Well, we know they are all together." Bandhu said reasonably. "And what harm could they possibly have come to?"

Nevertheless, every passing police car or ambulance going by with its siren on had the men on edge. There did seem to be a lot of emergency vehicles for the time of night.

At first, all the men sat together in Mahir's car, which was the roomiest as he had two children and a mother-in-law to convey around. He had been tapping his fingers against the steering wheel every now and again while Adam, who was in the front passenger seat, was listening to music. Bandhu, Mohal and Nayan had been in the back, looking at their phones, as if the answer to the whereabouts of the young women would lie there. In the end, Mahir's tapping, and the beat from Adam's earphones, had got too much, which is when Mohal had suggested they get some air.

"Nothing on social media." Mohal reported to the group loitering by the cars. "No local news which might involve them."

"They probably had such a good time they left later than they thought they would". Mahir tried to lift their spirits.

"Let's hope we organise the stag do better." Adam muttered. It wasn't scheduled to happen until nearer the time of the wedding, but it was all in the timetable they had been given by the wedding planner. Only she hadn't foreseen that the young women might go AWOL if let out on their own like this.

The September night was starting to turn a little damp and the air was getting heavy. Possibly it would turn to mist or fog by morning, which was not uncommon in the autumn. Sometimes the fog hardly seemed to lift, it just crept to the edges of the day and then returned as night fell. Mahir, who had checked the weather report while in his car, was beginning to worry a little, but he did not want to frighten the others. There was a strong chance of a shower. The girls had hardly been dressed for rain. What if they had got stuck outside somewhere?

"Should we tell your mother?" Mahir asked Mohal. "I was thinking it might be better to forewarn her." Knowing his boss at the dental surgery he realised she would not be asleep, for all her protestations that she would be getting an early night. Padma would be lying awake waiting to hear her daughter returned safely to the family home, which was where she would spend the night.

"No!" Mohal answered sharply. "There's no point worrying her unnecessarily" he added. "She'll only exaggerate it in her mind. Better to wait 'til we have the full story."

"OK" Mahir conceded, checking the time. "They are well over an hour late, though. We should do something soon."

"Such as what?" Adam had taken off his earphones to make this interjection. "Should we ask on social media if anyone has info?" Adam's job in brand representation involved promotion on various social media platforms. It seemed the obvious step to him.

"Don't want to worry anyone." Mohal spoke, shaking his head "And the girls won't thank us for raising the alarm unnecessarily" he added, thinking how mad Rita would be if they showed they had been worried.

Just as Adam took in a breath and prepared to argue the opposite case, a police van entered the car park. To the surprise of the men who were standing around, the police van carried on driving towards them and stopped across the bonnet of the Bandhu's golden-brown coloured Dacia Duster. As Nayan concernedly exited Mahir's car, two uniformed officers jumped out of the front seat of the van. One went to the side and slid open the door. Then the men who had been waiting saw the reason for this arrival.

Six bedraggled young women were helped from the van, one still wearing a piece of white lace in her hair masquerading as a wedding veil. On top of their pink T-shirts, they now had round their shoulders foil blankets, like the ones you saw worn by marathon runners after a race.

The men hurried over to the group of women.

"What happened?" Mohal was the first to speak.

"A fire" Ayeesha said to their alarm.

"Where? At the restaurant?" Mahir asked.

"No. We were walking back towards New Walk" she omitted reference to the conga, "There was a house which was on fire."

Morwenna, often not the most articulate of people, found her voice too. "The smoke was quite dense." she said and began to cough rather dramatically as if to prove it.

"There was a man in the house" Priya starting to tell Mohal, "He was calling for help. Rita was so brave. She covered her face with her pink T-shirt and ran into the smoke."

Mahir looked concerned. Mohal shook his head, "Oh Rita" he wailed, "I wish you wouldn't do these things. What will I tell our mum?"

"Don't tell her anything!" Rita pleaded, "Or just say we helped get someone out of a house fire. She's bound to notice the smell."

"Yes, you do stink a bit!" Mahir agreed.

"I expect the man was grateful?" Mohal asked, his journalistic instinct kicking in. What was the story here he was wondering? Could he use it for his vlog?

"That was an odd thing." Priya was saying, "Rita helped him out of the house. We sat him on the pavement. We were trying to make sure he was OK, and talking to the emergency services on the phone so they could assess his medical condition. But as soon as we heard the siren of the fire engine, would you believe it, he just took off!"

"So much for gratitude" said Bandhu, who was still appraising the state of his daughters and wondering what their mother would say.

"What do you mean, took off?" Mohal pursued.

"He just, like, got up off the pavement, where I was examining him, and ran off. I've never seen anything like it. Not even in A&E." Priya said. "I'm sure he was having severe respiratory problems, because of the smoke, but he still managed to escape."

"When the police and the fire brigade arrived, all we could do was describe him." Shona put in.

"At least we could tell them not to bother with the

ambulance." Shreya added.

"What about the six of you? Are they really OK?" Mahir addressed his last question to the two police officers.

"They were checked over at the scene by the paramedics" the first officer said, "They were cleared to go home, but do go to A&E if your breathing gets worse or you have any other symptoms." He addressed this last remark to the young women, especially to Morwenna who had stopped coughing at last.

"And thanks for your help." the second officer said. "We have your details and we'll be in touch if we need more information. Now I suggest you get in the warm and have a hot drink when you get home."

The half-dozen tired women nodded and moved towards the parked cars as the police van drew away from the car park.

Morwenna, and Ayeesha climbed into the back of Adam's car. He would take them back to the flat in Freemens Meadow ,where Rita usually lived. They gave feeble waves to their friends. "Message me in the morning." Morwenna said.

Saturday 21st September 2019 12.45 am

Nayan, Rita and Priya got into Mohal's car. Shona and Shreya, looking weary, slid into Bandhu's vehicle for a lift home. Mahir said his goodbyes and headed for his home in Syston.

Everyone in Mohal's car was quiet for a bit. Mohal was trying to make sense of the story the girls had told. It did not take long to reach the roundabout and he took the Oadby exit, noticing how little traffic there was at this time of night. In the early evening you could queue at that junction for ages.

"Did they know who the man in the house might have been?" Mohal queried as he turned into Elm Drive.

In his rear-view mirror, he saw his sister shrug.

"The police were trying to find out who was in the house

- I guess they won't make much progress 'til morning." Rita told him. "From what I overheard, it seems like the property was rented to a well-known operator. Someone who rents on behalf of others, then sublets. The owner is none the wiser provided the rent is paid. All sorts of things happen on those kinds of properties apparently, prostitution, people trafficking, cannabis farms."

Mohal nodded, wondering how much of this he could use in his vlog.

"Why was the house on fire?" Nayan in the passenger seat was talking excitedly, he could not keep his thoughts to himself. "Houses don't catch fire by themselves, do they? Trust you, Rita, to get involved with a burning house! I mean, I ask you! You are always around when there's trouble. Remember that man who died on the train?"

Driving in his car, Mahir had been thinking the same thing. He was recalling the dead man on the train, and other incidents, when Rita's fate had been too close to call. He knew in his heart that she would always be like this. But it did not make him any less afraid for her. Somehow mystery seemed to follow her and she had to try to solve it.

Saturday 21st September 2019 1.00 am

Arriving at 10 Elm Drive, the four figures gathered on the drive for a few moments.

"It was seriously weird. More than just a bit of subletting" Priya said to Mohal.

"What d' you mean?" Mohal wanted to know everything before they got in the house and had to play things down for their mother's benefit. Not that the four of them having a discussion on the driveway would not look suspicious if she looked out.

"I thought I saw someone else, someone lying on the floor, under a wardrobe" Rita explained, "I saw their legs and feet.

But the man I was helping shook his head. 'No, no, no one there' he kept repeating. I told the fire officer this and they went to check."

"You'll never guess what he came out of the house with!" Priya put in. The four of them were now standing in a tight ring. If Padma looked out, she would definitely sense something was going on.

"A firefighter came out carrying them. Two legs I mean. They were half covered by a tarpaulin." she told the astonished brothers.

"What do you mean, legs?" Mohal was puzzled. "Like the legs of a model you mean? A sculpture or a mannequin?"

"Oh no" Priya said, and Rita nodded at her, "They were real enough."

"I don't get it." Mohal said.

"Neither did anyone who was there," Rita told them. "When we left, the fire had been put out and the police scene of crimes team was coming. They put a white tent outside the house at the front door."

"In case they found any more legs?" Mohal asked, half joking.

"Or other body parts, I guess" Priya replied seriously.

"The legs must have belonged to a body and a head once." Rita said sombrely. The fire incident had drained all the fun from the evening. "And the man I rescued knew it wasn't a person any more. I'm sure of it. He didn't want us to go back in. And as soon as he could he ran off."

"So, what was he doing in the house with bits of a body. What's your guess?" Priya puzzled.

"Sounds like he might have been trying to get rid of a body. Maybe by starting a fire and it got out of control? That's my theory." Mohal was pleased with this scenario. It seemed to fit the facts.

"So that's why the police may want to speak to you all again?" Nayan said. "I think the less we tell Mum the better."

Chapter

18

"Later still, the war memorials would sprout from the earth, dwelling not on the loss, but on what the loss had won, and what a fine thing it was to be victorious. 'Victorious and dead,' some muttered, 'is a poor sort of victory."'

M. L. Steadman

Sunday 29th December 2019 3.00 pm

Before Nayan got to Dev's again, Jamie Bridge, a half-eaten croissant crumbled on the plate in front of him, had been chewing over the mystery of the head in the Cathedral.

At first, the force feared the head might be connected to a terrorist attack. The officers in the patrol car which attended when the 999 call was made had alerted the counter terrorism squad before taking care of scene management and making sure everyone stayed well away for their own safety. With nothing to go on, there was a concern that someone might have left the head as a decoy and there could be a bomb on the premises. Leicester Cathedral might not be the largest, or most glamorous, in the country, but it served as a symbol to the city, and had played an important role in its recent claim to fame when the body of Richard III was reinterred there. Having it damaged in an explosion was unthinkable.

The area surrounding the cathedral was cordoned off, and it, together with the nearby Richard III Visitor Centre, was visited by sniffer dogs and their handlers, with no result. While counter terrorism detectives continued their work, checking whether there was a connection with anyone on the watch list, Jamie Bridge and his team were tasked with exploring other lines of inquiry. Someone mentally disturbed, perhaps, or motivated by revenge? In the absence of any clues as to who had left the head, the only place they could start was with the person who had found it.

Having satisfied themselves that the building was clean, the police set about interviewing the cathedral staff in a room at the Visitor Centre, that being a convenient location for the witnesses. "Let the mountain come to Muhammad" DC Yousef Mohamed, who had studied Francis Bacon at university and liked to quote him, said as he walked through the automatic doors with his DCI, smiling at the police officer on the reception desk. When they got to the interview room, which was usually used as an education centre and was decorated with pictures of the Battle of Bosworth, the verger was sipping a plastic cup of sweetened tea. She was still wearing her black gown, which was like an academic gown, over a black jumper and skirt. Her hand shook as she raised the cup to her lips.

Maria Pettyfer explained her role as Head Verger was to help to organise the religious services, to make sure everything ran smoothly for the clergy who would conduct them. "I arrived as usual about 4.15pm," she told them, "to set up for evensong, that's the evening service, at 5. 30pm. Visitors are required to leave by 5pm." The verger looked up for a moment, checking they had understood and prepared to elaborate further. She was used to taking groups of youngsters round the cathedral and explaining the daily rhythm of services which took place there. Many were surprised to hear about this, being under the impression that churches and cathedrals were used on Sundays only.

Jamie Bridge nodded, encouraging her to go on at her own pace. He had found with witnesses it was best to let them tell the story in their way, and their own words, the first time. You could go back over it and check details later if necessary. Let them tell the story while it was as fresh as it could be in their memory, bearing in mind that the human memory was fickle, and details that witnesses were convinced about could be misremembered even a short time after the event. Sometimes the mind recalled what it wanted to have seen, sometimes the discrepancies, like the colour of a car or the age of a perpetrator, were beyond explanation.

Maria Pettyfer, was in her late forties, the DCI judged, although her hair, which she kept short, was completely white, giving her a slightly ethereal appearance. She sat very upright in the chair and appeared to have a tall, willowy build. She would command respect in the cathedral's precincts he thought. She came across as sensible and practical. Hopefully she had noticed something useful, he thought. Eventually, they would get to the rest of the staff, which might include the Bishop, he thought, swallowing hard at the prospect. He had never met a Bishop before.

Mrs Pettyfer was speaking. "It's a question of making sure the visitors - the tourists - the ones who come to see Richard III's tomb – know when the service starts and invite them to leave, unless they are attending."

"And today?" DC Mohamed seemed keen to get into the narrative about the discovery of the head. Jamie Bridge gave him a slightly disapproving look.

The verger put her plastic cup back on the table. "We tidy up and put out the service cards, and we also carry out a basic security check. We're not trained like you," she acknowledged, "but we look for anything suspicious. Mostly, it's bags left behind by accident. I found a complete picnic lunch once, inside a lovely basket, and once someone left their baby's car seat, but thankfully there was no baby in it."

"What did you find today, Mrs Pettyfer?" the Detective Constable pressed, getting another stare from his boss. DC Mohamed was clearly getting impatient, and this was only the first interview they had to do.

"As I approached the crossing, that's the central area where the north and south transepts intersect with the chancel which extends east and the nave which stretches west." Yousef and Jamie nodded in unison. The exact architectural term and its meaning were not that important to them but they had seen a plan of the building. "I could see there was a bag, a carrier bag, Sainsbury's it was, one of those orange ones, lying under a chair. We aren't supposed to use plastic carriers so much now are we? Not with all this concern about climate change. But they still come in useful, as in this case I suppose..."

The verger's voice tailed off and she stared into the distance. Yousef sighed and tapped his pen on the notepad he had brought into the interview/education room. He had not written very much so far.

"Well I looked at the bag before I touched it. Just in case it wasn't what I thought, you know?" the verger looked at the two officers for reassurance. They nodded their confirmation that this had been the right thing to do.

"There was something about it. Perhaps because it seemed to contain a round shape. I thought maybe a football..." her voice tailed off again as she recalled the horror of what she had found when she opened the handles of the bag and peered inside.

"So, you picked up the bag?" the constable prompted.

Mrs Pettyfer shivered. "Yes, I took it by the handles, picked it up from under the chair and I stood up. It was heavier than I expected, I suppose... I opened the bag. And inside I saw.. I saw.."

The police officers nodded. The verger did not need to describe the contents. They had seen the pictures.

"I suppose I froze for a couple of seconds. My brain was trying to tell me it wasn't real, that it was a model or something. Then Jeff, the security guard, came running towards me. He'd seen what I'd done, I think. He told me to put the bag down, which I did, and then we both stepped away and he called you."

"Mmmn" DC Mohamed said, keen to ask the rest of his questions.

But the verger was in full flow now. "I don't think I'll ever forget it. Someone's head…It wasn't like one of those reconstructions they do in labs. They did one for Richard III, you know. To see what he might have looked like." she was rambling now. "It was based on the remains they found in the car park."

"And you and Jeff cleared the cathedral and looked out for any more parcels?" DC Mohamed took the story forward.

"Yes." Maria Pettyfer said shortly. DCI Bridge had been afraid of this. If pushed at the wrong pace she might clam up.

"Can I take you back to before you found the bag." he tried. "Did you see anything to arouse suspicion from the moment you got to the cathedral? Anyone acting oddly?"

The verger was staring into the distance again. Presumably, she was still mesmerised by the thought of what she had seen in the plastic bag.

"Mrs Pettyfer?" he prompted gently.

"Oh. Well. No." she spoke succinctly. "At least I don't think so." she frowned as if trying to envision what had happened in the time before she saw the bag. The interviewers could see it wasn't easy. The discovery had clearly been a great shock.

"The only thing that stands out is that as I went into the cathedral someone was coming out. Not the usual type of person, but I don't want to judge."

"What sort of person do you usually see?" the constable put in unhelpfully at that point.

"Well, as I said, we get a lot of visitors. Many of them are foreign, Americans especially. There's a strong Richard III society over there. And the Herrick family, who migrated to the US, have given money to the cathedral and have a chapel named after them. Visitors tend to be in couples or families or, if they are on their own, they often carry a camera or a guide. Then there are the worshippers. Some come to pray. That's mostly at lunchtime. Workers come in to light a candle for someone. In the afternoon we get the odd shopper who stops off to see us."

"So, what stood out about this particular person?" Jamie Bridge leant forward. This might be the only lead they had.

"I don't know, really." was the verger's unpromising start. "He was on his own, he was Asian, which is neither here nor there of course, but Asian men tend to come with wives or families. He didn't have any of the tourist paraphernalia with him. He wasn't carrying a bag."

"Was there anything distinguishing about him?" the DCI probed with trepidation. So far, the man could be one of tens of thousands of people in Leicester alone.

"Mmmn" Mrs Pettyfer shut her eyes for a moment, then opened them. "He was wearing a yellow coat." She said, "and he had an earring – well they all have them these days, don't they? He only had one,though. It was in his right ear lobe. An interesting elephant design."

* * *

Leaning his elbow on the plastic table cloth provided by Dev's deli, Jamie Bridge sighed and took out a notebook from his jacket pocket, checking his new pay-as-you-go phone as he did this in case there was a message from Superintendent Turner or his team. The DCI made a note - 'Elephant earring?'

Where had he seen one of those recently? DC Mohamed had conducted the rest of the interviews for Inspector Lu, who took over the investigation (or 'headed it up' as Nayan had joked with Jamie Bridge). He was kept busy at tactical planning meetings for the factory surveillance. So, Jamie Bridge never met the Dean, the most senior cleric on the scene that day, he later learned. He had managed to skim through the interview reports in between his other tasks. He had not given the reports much attention, he had to concede. Now he thought about it, he could not recall the earring being mentioned in them, or that the DC had raised the question of this visitor who the verger had mentioned with the other interviewees. Was that the case, and if so why? If only he was allowed back in the office, he could chase this up.

Sunday 29th December 2019 11.00 pm

Rita had been sitting on the sofa all day. Her captors had not bothered to make her lie down or use the blankets. In fact, she hadn't seen much of them for the last few hours, not since the police dropped off an Indian meal from a local deli. It wasn't bad, Rita thought, but not as good as her mum's cooking. Really, Colin was using the police like Deliveroo, the takeaway delivery service that Nayan had worked with for a while, before he got tired of cycling round Leicester with a huge pack of other peoples' meals on his back.

She might have been tempted to make a dash for the door downstairs, were it not for the gun. She was still unsure whether there were other people in the building, apart from Colin, Anya and Jai. She could bump into one of them, if so. Also, it was pretty clear that Colin and Jai, at least, were in the corridor just outside the room where she was being held, because she could hear them shouting. At one point Colin said, "Just get it done!" It reminded Rita of the team building weekend the legal firm had organised at Melton Mowbray in Leicestershire, during which Domenico from Accounts had used pretty much the same words as they tried to guide blindfolded members of staff through a maze. Rita had preferred the afternoon sessions on 'gourmet challenge' and 'creative canapes', as a nod to the foodstuffs for which Melton Mowbray was famous. At least no one shouted while she was balancing an olive on a cheese-filled pastry case.

It was as if her captors were preparing for something big.

Rita decided to pull the blankets over herself and try to get some sleep. Whatever the 'big thing' was, she doubted it would be good news for her.

Chapter

19

"That great Cathedral space which was childhood."
Virginia Woolf

Monday 30th December 2019 1.00 am

Sleep would only come in short bursts. It was as if, spending a third night on the couch, her body was in a state of alarm and would not let her rest for long. She could feel herself beginning to despair. Would she ever escape? She was longing to see Mahir again. She missed him so much. She was lying in an uncomfortable position, with blankets that kept sliding off her, trying to conjure up some sleep. Listening to Colin's snores on the chair opposite, Rita realised she was twisting the ring on her finger, which at least brought back happy thoughts.

Thursday 31st January 2019 9.00 pm

"We'll go to a country hotel." Mahir had said, "Pamper ourselves." It sounded like just the relaxing break she needed, Rita thought, looking down at her broken nails and cracked hands. Before helping to run the B&B for Athena, she had never used them so much. By the time she'd done the cleaning to cover when the cleaner was off (which was often), and kept the kitchen tidy for breakfasts, it was time to replenish the shelves of the shop and to sweep outside. Her fingers seemed constantly to be in rubber gloves or touching bin bags. It would be lovely to have her hands back again she thought.

In her room, Rita looked critically at the clothes she had brought with her. She had packed to be practical, not to eat in a nice hotel somewhere. Perhaps her black pinafore would do if she found something to wear with it?

"You're not going in that!" had been Athena's reaction when she mentioned it. "Take the afternoon off. If the shop is stocked I can manage. Have a wander round the shops – you haven't done much of that. Find something really nice to wear!" she said it like it was an order, "You can borrow shoes and jewellery from me." Athena added. She seemed to be looking forward to Rita's treat weekend almost as much as she was. "And don't worry about me while you're away with Mahir. There's only one booking and they are regulars, so they'll muck in if I get tired."

So, there she found herself, sitting at a table in the dining room of the five-star Lympstone Manor Hotel, thinking Priya won't believe this when I tell her! Mahir had clearly gone to a lot of trouble. He had picked her up at 6pm in his white car, wearing his dinner suit which made him look so handsome, and his hair had been freshly cut at the barber's. "I thought you were supposed to be at a dentists' conference?" Rita said after they had hugged and she had smelt his aftershave.

"There was a gap in the programme!" he joked. "Your mum was cool about me leaving early, seeing as it involved you." he smiled at her. As the car pulled away from the guest house, Rita thought she caught sight of Athena waving from the sitting room window.

The Michelin Star restaurant, run by Michael Caines under the motto "After love there is only cuisine", looked out over the Exe estuary which leant it a tranquil atmosphere. The sunset over the river could be spectacular, Rita knew, everywhere bathed in an orange glow. Tonight, the dark water was illuminated by the reflections of bright silver moonlight. The moon had been pretty spectacular, recently, as Rita's brother had pointed out to her. Ten days ago, it had been extra large in the sky and Nayan had called it a super moon.

Rita and Mahir were seated on blue chairs at a table covered by an immaculately white cloth. They had been led to a place by the window from where they could see the lights of boats twinkling as they bobbed in the water. The restaurant was quietly busy. There were a few other couples, some of whom might be locals, and a group of six who looked like they were celebrating a parent's birthday. The hotel had extensive grounds, it seemed, and they were promised a tour of the vineyard tomorrow. Everything was the height of luxury. Rita had not been able to believe how plush the room was, when they had checked in and left their luggage before heading down to eat. It put the guest house in the shade, that was for sure. Athena had been right; her pinafore would not have cut it here.

Rita had not had time to explore much of the town of Totnes when she went on her shopping trip, being preoccupied with Athena and her business. The narrow historic streets, lined with shops and cafes, reminded her a little of York, which she had visited with Priya. She guessed it must be the medieval buildings, which jostled alongside each other, some with bays and shop fronts sticking out into the street. She hoped, before she left, to be able to take a ferry trip along the river Dart, on the banks of which the historic market town was situated, overseen by a Norman motte and bailey castle, built to keep the Anglos Saxons under control after the Conquest.

The dress she had found had Athena's approval when she returned. It was knee length, with a high neck, short sleeves, a cinched waist and a bow at the back. The blue shade suited Rita, and Athena ran to fetch her a pair of blue topaz droplet stud earrings, far nicer than any Rita usually wore, and some blue kitten heel shoes, which Rita wasn't sure she could walk in. The blue sequin evening bag she had found on eBay was sitting beside her place at the table and the cashmere pashmina, also from eBay, was folded on the back of her chair. She did not need it now but it might be useful if they took a stroll outside after the meal. Rita's hair was tidy for once, piled up neatly on top of her head thanks to Athena.

They had eaten well, with lots of vegetarian options to supplement the menu. Even so, the raspberry souffle was taking a long time to arrive, Rita thought. Mahir was talking about his plans. He told her how he hoped to run his own dental clinic before long, and he thought that would be in Leicester, as that would give his children stability, but wanted to know if Rita planned to stay in Leicester too? "Because that would matter to me," he said quietly and seriously, taking her hand.

"Of course, I want to stay there!" Rita had protested, smiling. "It's my home." she said. "My mum is there, and my brothers will always be there, even if they leave, they'll come back, and it's not too far to visit Priya and who knows where she will practice once she qualifies as a doctor.."

"Rita, be quiet" she had got so carried away with thinking about the future she had not realised that Mahir had risen from the table and was kneeling beside her. What was the matter? Had she dropped her napkin? No, she became aware that everyone else in the restaurant was looking at them while trying to pretend not to. Forks were poised between plate and mouth. The waiters had stopped moving.

Mahir took a box from his pocket and from the box he took a ring.

"I want to be with you for the rest of my life" Mahir said looking straight into her eyes, "Will you marry me Rita?"

Monday 30th December 2019 1.00am

Rita's eyes welled up, as they did every time she thought of it. The effort he had made, the beautiful ring she could feel on her finger now, the hush of the restaurant followed by the applause when she fell on his neck, had made a deep impression.

"Of course I will!" she had whispered "I can't imagine life without you."

Monday 30th December 2019 11.00 am

Rita had woken from a disturbed night. After a breakfast of digestive biscuits and mint tea, she splashed cold water on her face as the best she could do for washing, staring at her round face with its snub nose in the cracked mirror above the basin. The mirror was not looking its best and neither was she. Even allowing for the distortions in the glass, her skin looked blotchy and there were bags under her eyes. Lack of sleep and living on take-away food was taking its toll. Sighing as she returned to the room, she had settled on a corner of the sofa to sit out another day. The atmosphere inside the factory was getting tense. Something was about to happen. Rita could sense it. Colin was in the corridor barking orders into his phone. He was near enough for her to guess from his tone what he was doing, but annoyingly too far away for her to gather the words he was saying.

It was very troubling. What would happen to her if they did not need her anymore? As far as she could tell, Colin and Jai had been stalling the police while they did something? What? Warn their associates? Not only was it worrying that Colin had a gun and was prepared to use it, as he had shown when he shot at her when she first arrived in the building, but she thought it highly likely that armed police were waiting outside. Rita had encountered armed police before. They didn't mess about. She thought back to the terrorist shot not so long ago on London Bridge, wearing a false suicide belt. The police had their protocols and they were trained to act in a certain way. Any sudden move could result in a blood bath.

Rita tried taking some deep breaths and rolling her shoulders. It did not seem to help much. She needed to relax.

There was nothing she could do to control the situation. She was desperate to see her family again. Would that ever happen? They had all been together so recently, it was hard to believe. It felt like a scene from another age. Rita cast her mind back to that last meal, when they had been so happy, before this trouble started.

Tuesday 24th December 2019 6.00 pm

"Why has she called us all together?" Nayan's voice spoke over the engine of Mohal's car as it laboured up Houghton Hill, always a challenge for the hybrid Mohal found. He had picked up his brother from Uppingham, a market town on the A47 between Leicester and Peterborough. Nayan and a friend had cycled there that afternoon.

"I dunno, bro" Mohal, hands on the wheel, shrugged his shoulders, "Perhaps she's got a new recipe innit?" he offered as a theory.

"We don't all need to be there for that!" Nayan was dismissive. "We've got her in a WhatsApp group now," he persisted, "Why can't she message us?" he asked, turning to look behind him to check his bike, which Mohal had loaded into the car, was surviving the journey.

"Askin' the wrong guy." Mohal smiled. As the eldest child he had learnt to accept his mother's strange ways. He tried not to fight them like his brother Nayan did. To be fair, he thought, it was easier now he was living away from home. Nayan was still there and in the thick of it.

"Priya coming?" Nayan asked, referring to Rita's best friend, who was having a rare break from her medical studies in Oxford.

"She's on her way" Mohal confirmed. "Rita's bringing her."

* * *

"What's your Mum up to?" Priya, in the passenger seat of Rita's car, queried, dipping her fingers into a packet of Haribo sweets. They were the ones without gelatine, which her brother-in-law had brought back from Belgium, she told her friend. Rita took in the fact that Jai had been abroad without comment, as Priya fed a sweet into her mouth.

"Your guess is as good as mine." Rita managed when the sweet had dissolved. She shook her head, loosening the scarf tied at the nape of her neck to retain her curly brown hair.

"You must be used to her by now" Rita added, checking her mirror and signalling to join the A46. "She likes to get us all together and, although she complains, she likes a bit of drama too."

Priya rolled her eyes and looked out of the window on her left. She wasn't sure Rita was right about her mother, not as to the second part, anyway. Rita had had plenty of drama in her life already and Padma hadn't seemed to enjoy any of it.

"She's bound to have cooked loads, so we shouldn't eat any more." Rita warned her friend when she was about to help themselves to more Haribo. Priya put the packet into her bag, took out a handwipe and used it to clean her fingers. She had not spent so many years on her doctor's training not to have learnt about germs and the importance of cleanliness. Only the other day, she had read an article about the lack of hygiene on airline seats that made her feel ill and definitely put her off the idea of flying. She'd mentioned it to Rita's brother, Mohal, who said bus seats were just as bad. Priya shuddered and patted down her brown black hair which lay smooth and straight, skimming the top of her shoulders.

* * *

Jaina, Padma's sister, and her husband, Bandhu, were sitting in silence as the Dacia Duster made its way to Oadby, both lost in their own thoughts. There was a further round of reselection going on at the Health Trust which was preoccupying Bandhu as he drove. He might not escape the cuts this time. It was like a never-ending game of musical chairs, he thought, except that as the chairs were removed the goal posts shifted as well (to mix his metaphors) so that what had represented 'excellence in delivery' last time round was considered a profligate waste of resources the next time. Customer satisfaction was less important than meeting targets, 'doing more with less' as the bosses liked to say. Austerity had been going on for so long it had become the new norm. The cracks were not just showing in all service areas, they were widening. Bin collections had been cut, schools were talking about closing on Fridays, the rate of youth crime, especially stabbings, was rising while youth centres closed, and libraries were being handed over to volunteers.

Jaina was worrying about their daughters, Shona and Shreya, and how they were doing with revision for their exams, which they would face as soon as they returned to university in the New Year. They had elected to stay in college for an extra fortnight, to Bandhu's horror when he saw the cost. Perhaps it would be cheaper when they moved out and into a house, he was beginning to think. Both had told her not to worry, but how could she not when, in their first term, one had broken her ankle and the other had lost her passport. They would be coming home in time for the wedding, they had assured her.

"They'll be fine." Bandhu said without taking his eyes off the road and without his wife saying a word. He knew what she was anxious about. "They'll be back in time." he added. Jaina stole a look at her husband under her eyelids as he continued to focus on the road. All very well for him, she thought, he never seemed to let anything annoy him. At least this family meal arranged by her sister would provide a distraction

"Stop looking at your phone all the time, Nayan!" Padma uttered crossly.

Nayan was checking what the football pundits thought, while also waiting to see if his eBay bid had been successful. Leicester City had just been beaten by Manchester City after a nine-match run without defeat. Was this the beginning of a slide down from their second position? Hopes had been high that they would play in Europe again next year if their form continued. The games over the Christmas and New Year period would be crucial. The bid was also crucial, as he had promised the goods to someone, with a mark-up of course. Success with the bid would give him a good profit.

"I have to, Mum, sorry." it was not a real apology. "It's for my new business. I'm buying and selling stuff on the internet, aren't I? Got to finance my studies somehow. As a post grad I've got more flexibility. I can keep an eye on my bids while I'm doing research. It beats zero hours jobs like I was doing before. Hospitality was the worst. It was mostly stacking and unstacking chairs, while wearing uncomfortable clothes and tight shoes."

Padma shook her head in an uncomprehending way. Her son did not know what real hard work was, she thought, looking back on the hours she had put in to qualify as a dentist, and at a time when few women, let alone from ethnic minority backgrounds, did so.

"Tell me about it." Morwenna, Rita's friend and flatmate who had been invited to the meal, put in. "At least you didn't have to wear a short skirt and get your bum pinched." She spoke from experience. Her few weeks of waitressing at events held at Leicester Race Course had taught her a lot about how to deter unwanted attention.

"Well, not the skirt bit anyway." Nayan said to everyone's surprise.

"None of you seem to have proper jobs anymore," Padma complained, "Well, apart from you, Rita," she beamed at her daughter, "You are going to be a solicitor, I know what one of those is. While you do your sales, whatever those are," she said looking at Nayan, "and you.." she gave her eldest, Mohal, a mystified look, "I don't know what you do, write to people on the internet?"

"It's a vlog, Mum," he sighed, having explained this before. "A sort of video diary. I'm hoping to get something together for YouTube, then I'll get way more followers, maybe I can even make a podcast."

"I have no idea what you are talking about!" Padma laughed.

"The current theme is Leicester Live. But I can do it about anywhere. I report on events as they happen. Like the local news I used to write about for the Leicester Mercury, only no one wants to buy a load of news on printed paper any more, especially as it will be out of date before it hits the streets." Mohal went on.

"I buy the Mercury" Padma protested "I like to read what's happening in the City. I don't mind if it's not exactly up to date."

The others round the table exchanged looks and raised their eyebrows, but no one contradicted her out loud.

"Some of the media outlets take up what I say, even ask me for background or pieces on local issues. The BBC paid me recently for a vox pop on City's loss to Man City at the Etihad, for example. It's modern life. Newsprint is on the way out."

"But I have copies of the Mercury at the surgery." Padma protested, "What would my patients read if it didn't exist?"

More looks were exchanged around the table. Rita coughed and reached for her water glass to hide a smile. They were all thinking the same thing. Everyone looked at their phones these days, didn't they? Just what Padma had been ticking off Nayan for doing. There seemed to be an intergenerational misunderstanding here.

Wednesday 24th December 2019 8.00 pm

The meal proceeded without phones, in deference to Padma. Everyone tried not to mention Shona and Shreya, as these were a cause of tension to Jaina, or the forthcoming wedding, as this was a cause of stress for Padma.

Nayan wanted to talk about anniversaries. "Last year was 100 years since the end of the First World War, this year is 80 years since the start of World War Two and 50 years since the moon landing!" he said. "How the world changes!"

Yes, and three years since the BREXIT vote, Rita thought. It had been easier to put people on the moon than arrange for the country to leave the European Union. While she could see that the majority had voted to leave, she was not sure they had bargained for the consequential dithering and vacillations of the politicians. The arguments and the facts had been lost in the fog created, along with many MPs' careers it seemed to her. The country seemed more divided than ever, and some people seemed to think it acceptable to hurl sexist and racist abuse. Boris Johnson had taken over from Theresa May as Prime Minister, but his election victory did not augur well for reconciliation, she felt. How could the country heal and come together? It was all very unsettling.

Nayan was still carrying on, as if he'd swallowed an encyclopaedia. Rita knew he checked up on these things for pub quizzes, which he had started going to. It was quite unlike him, but he was moving in different circles now and taking up new interests. "In 1919 we were in the middle of the Spanish flu epidemic, which claimed 228,000 lives in Britain. They called it Spanish because Spain was particularly hard hit. We have antibiotics now, so it couldn't happen again."

"1919 was the year that Leicester regained city status" Rita put in, "We had been a city until we lost our Bishop in the eleventh century. We got it back for our efforts in World War One. It was also the year of the first two minutes silence for the war, and 1919 saw the first woman MP, lady Astor, take her seat in Parliament. There are people alive now who were living then. Just think of all the changes in their lifetime!" Rita was getting into it now. "Go back two hundred years and 1819 saw the Peterloo massacre" she added, "When our own troops opened fire on people protesting about lack of work."

"It's only a hundred years since Amritsar, of course." Mohal said quietly. He had covered the anniversary in his vlog and feelings about it were still raw. "Thousands had gathered in a public garden. The local commander ordered the entrances to be sealed and opened fire on the peaceful protesters. The official death toll was 379 with 1200 injured, but the real figures are probably much higher."

Rita nodded. The event had ignited Indian nationalism and provided recruits for Gandhi's independence movement, although it would take nearly another 30 years and another world war before this was achieved.

"Have we all had enough to eat?" Padma broke into the discussion.

Everyone nodded. They had eaten all they could manage of Padma's new recipes and declared all her dishes a success. They sat back from the table, waiting for her to say it was time to clear the plates away. But, instead, their mother stood up, a glass of fruit juice in her hand. Was she going to make a speech? Nayan thought. This would be a first.

"Thank you all for coming." Padma said seriously. Nayan put down his phone - his bid had been successful - and listened. This sounded important. "First of all, of course, we have the wedding to look forward to. I shall be losing a child but gaining another member of the family." She beamed at all those gathered round the table. Jaina winced slightly. She felt it very much that neither of her daughters seemed to be anywhere in the marriage stakes. She would love to be planning a wedding. "But I also wanted to announce…" Mohal looked at Rita, what was going on? Rita shook her head and raised her eyebrows. She was as surprised as he was.

"I wanted to announce that I am going to be leaving the dental practice."

"What?" Bandhu exclaimed.

"Why?" Jaina asked, concerned. "There's nothing wrong is there?"

"No, there is not. I just feel that this is the right time to step back, especially as it is my intention," she paused a moment, "to hand over the practice to Mahir, who will make an excellent job of it, I'm sure."

Mahir smiled modestly. He was the only one around the table who had had an inkling of this. It was a great privilege and responsibility, he said, rising to his feet and calling for a toast to Padma.

"To you Mum!" Rita beamed, seeing how happy Mahir was.

Chapter

20

"It is my conviction that killing under the cloak of war is nothing but an act of murder."

Albert Einstein

Monday 30th December 2019 12.00 pm

"Don't shoot! Don't shoot!" Colin shouted urgently into Rita's phone.

"We're coming out."

Broken from her memories, Rita had been told to get up and move quickly. Just like that. After days of sitting still, the act of moving so fast was dizzying. It had happened so quickly; she had no time to collect her thoughts. The four of them, Jai and Rita, Colin and Anya, were suddenly gathered in the lobby where Rita had first entered the building.

"Put these on!" Colin had commanded before they descended the stairs. Now they were all dressed in the same black outfits. What was he planning? Rita wondered.

* * *

Outside the disused factory, Sue Foster was directing operations, liaising with the unarmed teams in the surrounding streets and with the group leader of the armed response team, the officers closest to the building. Armed police were positioned behind the vans which they had parked opposite the factory entrance. In the next street were several patrol cars and an ambulance. The area had been cleared of civilians to avoid extra casualties. Bullets were hard to control and could ricochet off buildings and vehicles in the heat of the moment. Now they were aware of its potential as a route in and out of the building, the part of the river adjacent to the property had been closed to traffic. Somewhere around Aylestone there was a gathering of irate boat owners mooring up and going nowhere.

The businesses which normally occupied the other offices in the converted warehouse, where the surveillance operation was being conducted, had been warned on Saturday to stay away for the foreseeable. You will be compensated, Trissey had told them when the astonished solicitors and accountants expressed outrage at this disruption. They were not people to cross, Trissey thought, picturing law suits against the police force in due course.

"Put in a claim to Leicestershire constabulary." she had said. Anything to get them off her back. The evacuation meant the police officers were free to come and go and to use the whole of the car park at the back of the offices, with marked and unmarked vehicles. The era of secrecy was over. The operation could not be more public, occupying a useful spot in local and national news over a period which normally lacked big stories, although rumours were brewing about the royal family, with various gossip columnists happy to fan the flames. It sounded like Prince Andrew was being cut adrift for associating with the wrong people, and something was awry with Harry and Meghan, but no one knew what. There was a lot of speculation.

Jamie Bridge was sitting in Dev's, sensing big things were going on, and unable to help. Trissey James had messaged him to expect action. The DCI's right foot was tapping up and down under the table where a cold cappuccino stared up at him. There was only so much coffee you could drink, he had discovered.

Back in the surveillance room, DC Trissey Adams was watching events on the monitors. The screens now included a view of the waterside approach to the factory. The camera had been installed a couple of nights ago, by an officer who was lowered to the factory roof from a police helicopter which had hovered above for a short time under the subterfuge of loud music to distract the hostage takers.

Trissey was listening on the comms system to Sue Foster's barked orders. They could do with the cool head of the DCI she thought. How much operational experience did the ACC really have? But she knew it wasn't her place to speak out. Hopefully DCI Bridge would be cleared and return to work very soon.

Sue Foster had put on a bullet proof vest when she left the surveillance suite, as they were calling it now. Trissey had watched her arrival near the factory on the monitors. Before she had climbed into one of the vans, the ACC had swaggered with her importance a little, the Detective Constable felt, as if she was Boadicea or something.

"Hold your fire, they're coming out!" Sue Foster told the leader of the armed response unit in reaction to the suspect's panicky-sounding phone call. It seemed the hostage takers had seen the light at last and were prepared to give up.

"Suspects coming out!" he relayed to his team. "Get ready to receive! The hostage may be with them. She is female, 5 feet 7inches, IC4, I remind you, so she should be distinguishable from the male suspects."

Trissey Adams could hear on the comms system the various armed officers acknowledging the instructions and forming themselves up so they knew who would take the lead in speaking to each suspect (who they called 1 and 2), who would keep their gun trained on each, the tell-tale red light usually a deterrent to anyone except a fanatic or someone who had determined to die by 'police suicide' as it was called. Another officer would check the hostage takers were disarmed when they were lying on the ground. Only then would the plain clothes team move in to make the arrests. After that, the suspects would be bundled into separate police vans, and driven to Enderby police station for processing and questioning. It could be a long shift she thought to herself.

They still had little idea of the scale of the operation. Who were Colin Shawcross and Jai Choudrie working for? How long it had been going on? The DCI, with time on his hands, had linked the savage death and decapitation of one of their informers with two similar incidents. It seemed the purpose of leaving informants' heads, conspicuously in three cathedrals across the country, was to send shock waves through the criminal community and deter others from providing intelligence. The locations of the heads suggested the gang had a wide reach across most of England at least. They had no evidence to link the two perpetrators in the building to those crimes, but they would face multiple charges, one of the most serious being the kidnapping and detention against her will of Rita Patel.

A separate police team and a paramedic had been briefed and were prepared to run to the hostage and give her whatever aid she needed. All the officers were hoping she was not wounded or hurt in any way. Medical assistance had been repeatedly offered, but it was consistently declined.

"Don't shoot! Don't shoot" Colin Shawcross's whiny tones again came over on the telecoms system, the link they had made with Rita's phone. All the conversations during the siege had been recorded and listened to, in order to assist in the negotiations and as evidence in the trial. Shawcross had done the talking, although on a few occasions the listeners thought they had picked up another male voice, presumably Jai Choudhrie.

"Everyone ready." Sue Foster said, authoritatively, as they taught you on the senior police officers' courses, Trissey thought wryly.

A loud crack broke through the silence.

Trissey James stood, transfixed at what she was seeing on

the screens, struggling to take it in. The big double wooden door had suddenly splintered and two very powerful motorbikes roared out of the building, heading straight for the police vans opposite.

"Shoot the tyres not the suspects." the armed response team leader commanded.

"We can't tell who's who.." he explained.

But just as his command had gone out, Trissey realised that, despite the gunshots she could hear, it must be too late. In an instant, the BMW motorbikes had squeezed through the gaps between the police vans and shot out of sight of the monitors. Where had they gone?

* * *

A constable had been posted in the middle of a cul-de-sac at the end of the road which ran parallel to the factory. The constable was standing at the point where there was a footbridge linking the road to a housing estate. The officer was wearing her hi vis jacket over her uniform to warn any members of the public walking from the houses of an incident ahead. She reported on the comms that two bikes had just swept past her and gone over the bridge. Each bike, as Trissey had seen, had a male driver and a female passenger, she reported. All four were wearing black leather bike gear and black boots. On their heads were helmets with their visors down. Even playing back the footage of the escape, and slowing it down, as Trissey did now, it was impossible to tell who was who.

Sue Foster was still issuing orders. She wanted the housing estate surrounded and road blocks set up to prevent the suspects from escaping. So much for the budget for this operation, Trissey Adams thought. Leaving another officer to watch the screens, although the point of them seemed to have been lost now, the Detective Constable ran out of the office building and towards the factory. She wanted to see the scene for herself so she could report back to the DCI. Trissey Adams flashed her ID at the constable standing on duty by the broken door of the factory and hastily donned blue shoe covers so as not to upset the SOCOs.

At last, belatedly, they would be able to see inside the building. Trissey found herself in a large lobby area. There was a smell of fuel in the air, which was not surprising since two bikes had been started up in that confined space. The metal cupboard which stood against the back wall had black smudges on it, presumably made by exhaust fumes. The only other item in the hallway was lying on the floor near the cupboard. Trissey Adams bent down to look at it but did not pick it up. She saw what it was. It was a phone in a turquoise phone cover. That was all that was left of Rita Patel. How was she going to break this to her boss, who was still suspended and worried about Rita? There was no way to track the kidnappers or the hostage now.

* * *

Back at the temporary HQ in the converted warehouse, Sue Foster's face was as red as the tomato soup in her cup, a speciality of Dev's Deli down the road.

"Do I have to take command myself?" the Chief Constable had asked her.

"No sir, we'll soon track them down." the ACC said with more conviction than she felt.

The helicopter was searching the estate into which the bikes had burrowed. It could be seen swooping and diving in the distance. The housing estate, built in the nineteen fifties, had a series of walkways between the streets so that it was impossible to predict which direction the bikes had taken. Being a residential area there were no council CCTV cameras. Officers were going door to door trying to find witnesses or footage from dashcams or domestic security cameras. The latter seemed unlikely. The residents had put a lot of investment into satellite dishes, not so much into personal security, from what Trissey Adams was hearing from the officers on the ground.

Some householders were willing to help, but had seen nothing. Others were hostile, objecting to the heavy police presence and unwilling to cooperate. All traffic patrols had been alerted to look out for the motor bikes, but the chances were that the suspects had managed to switch vehicles. They were dealing with a highly sophisticated operation and the police were playing catch-up.

Monday 30th December 2019 4.00 pm

Early in the course of the surveillance, DC Trissey Adams had made good friends with the owner of Dev's, the Indian café, delicatessen and takeaway down the road from the offices where the operational room had been set up. She had ferried food frequently to officers on surveillance and encouraged them to use the establishment too. Curries and rice were ordered at all hours in the afternoon and evening, bacon rolls in the morning. The officers even bought hot drinks, even though the offices they were using had a kettle and plenty of mugs.

Trissey Adams had been specifically chosen by Jamie Bridge for this operation. He had seen her potential and wanted to encourage the young constable. Although she looked slight compared to her fellow officers, Trissey was tough, he had found, and showed a lot of initiative. Just what the modern force needed. Trissey had moved to Leicester from Trinidad in her late teens, sensing that her career prospects would be better in the UK. Her only regret, as she frequently told other officers, was in choosing a place so far from the sea. She missed the ocean, which had been the backdrop of her childhood and Leicester was about as far as you could be from any coastline in the UK, she discovered. Still, she appreciated the multicultural vibe of the city and there was a strong Caribbean community. The annual Caribbean festival was well attended and the sort of fruits and vegetables she had been used to eating at home were easy to get hold of. That went some way to make up for the lack of sunshine, she supposed. In her late twenties now, she hoped to emulate her boss and rise in the ranks. She felt she could learn a lot from Jamie Bridge.

Since the DCI's suspension, Trissey's trips the trips to Dev's were coming in useful. It gave Trissey a chance to brief Jamie Bridge who, he assured her, was blameless of the accusations against him. While she waited for the take-way food to be prepared, the Detective Constable sat at a table with DCI Bridge and brought him up to date with what she had seen in the lobby of the factory. He agreed with her that finding Rita's phone was a blow. The suspects would have got away from the housing estate within minutes, he guessed. It was like looking for a needle in a haystack, Jamie Bridge thought.

"But the bikes? How did they get through the cordon?" he asked, passing his hand through the ginger stubble of his closely shaved head. He had passed the hair clipper over it a second time the previous evening, in honour of the penance he was undergoing.

Trissey cleared her throat "Well, they hadn't been too clever there, guv." she said quietly, checking no one was around to overhear. "The armed officers were drawn up behind the vans which were parked lengthways, bonnets pointing to the road, in case they needed to leave quickly. They're always being called to emergencies. There was a gap between the vehicles, so the armed officers could get in and out. A gap just wide enough for a motorbike. The guns were trained on the factory door, expecting people to walk out.

By the time they refocussed on the bikes bursting out of the door, the bikes were on them and too close to fire safely, really." Trissey told her boss, watching him shake his head in disbelief and frustration. Jamie Bridge curled his right hand into a fist and hit the table with it, causing the proprietor of the cafe to look up in alarm. The DCI was thinking that he should have been there! He might have seen the danger.

"A couple of officers fired after the bikes sped past, aiming for the tyres like the skipper said, but it was too late." the constable told him.

"And Rita Patel?" Jamie Bridge was trying to breathe calmly and stop thoughts of strangling Sue Foster from surfacing in his mind. What was he going to tell Nayan?

"There were four people on the bikes." Trissey told him. "A man and a woman on each bike."

"Four people? How?" the DCI was confused. Assuming one of the figures was Rita, when had the other woman got into the building, and who was she?

"Don't know sir. Our intelligence hasn't been the greatest, obviously, not since the head turned up..well.. you know" she did not need to finish the explanation. "They all had bike leathers on." she continued, "I looked closely at the footage. You just couldn't tell which was the hostage. In their helmets the women passengers looked the same!"

"Do we know who the other woman is? She's not another hostage?" Jamie Bridge asked.

"Inquiries are continuing." the Detective Constable said, "But it's looking possible that she is Chewbacca's wife. At least, she's not at the family home, and the children have gone abroad with an aunt."

"So, there was more the informer could have told us!" the DCI said, exasperated. Then he changed the subject. "I have to ask you, Trissey, what happened when you and Yousef cased the factory after the tip off?"

"I'm sorry," the DC began worryingly, then she continued,

"Yousef played me. He sent me to check out the surrounding streets while he went round the outside of the building. I should have gone with him, I know, but we were short of time and there were only the two of us. We had to get the cameras in place before Chewbacca got there."

"So, Yousef..?" Jamie Bridge began.

"Yes, 'fraid so, guv." Trissey Adams sighed, "He's been pulled in by Professional Standards. It's looking like he was the leak."

DCI Bridge groaned and put his head in his hands for a moment. "Damn!" he said, then "Sorry, it's just so disappointing. And it's keeping me from doing my job! Professional Standards are doing the criminals' work for them!"

"Mmmn" Trissey Adams rose from the table to collect the take-aways. "You'll be back soon I'm sure." She reassured her boss as she left Dev's, where the aroma of freshly made curry was making the DCI feel hungry. He needed to get back to work soon, he thought, if only for the sake of his waistline.

Chapter

21

"We shape our buildings; thereafter they shape us."
                                    Winston Churchill

Monday 30th December 2019 4.00pm

Rita felt the van slowing down. She heard the back door being opened. Two strong arms lifted her up and carried her out, putting her on her feet. "You'll be fine." an unknown male voice said. She heard the van roar off. Where was she? Rita took off the blindfold to see.

The very last rays of the sun were disappearing over the horizon in a flash of deep orange. She had better get going before it got completely dark, she thought, looking to right and left for clues as to where to head. The ground under her feet felt like gravel and she realised she was in a lay-by, or turning place, not far from a main road. As she accustomed her eyes, she could see traffic there. She was near an A road, not a motorway, which should make things easier. With no money and no phone, she wondered how to get help. She was still wearing the bike leathers, perhaps a motorist would take pity, thinking her bike had broken down?

There were no houses near the lay-by, as far as she could see. Across the road she could make out an area of woodland. The bare tree branches made patterns against the reddened sky which she would love to have admired if she wasn't in this predicament. The tops of the branches looked like fingers pointing upwards. Which way should she point herself?

To her left, she thought there might be a roundabout and beyond that, in the far distance, a set of traffic lights was going through its pattern of colours. If she wanted to attract the attention of a driver, it might be tricky if they were concentrating on the roundabout or the lights, she determined, so she turned to her right, walking along the edge of the lay-by until she reached the road. There was no pavement, she realised, and she would have to walk on grass, which was not easy as earlier rain had made it damp and slippery, even in her trainers. Her idea had been to walk facing the oncoming traffic and hail a friendly driver. But the speed of the traffic and slippery underfoot conditions were making her think again. She would have to go to the other side, where it looked as though there might be a more solid surface to walk on. Perhaps someone would see her crossing the road and stop to pick her up?

They didn't. Rita waited for a gap and crossed to the middle of the road, stood with bated breath hoping that in her black clothes the cars would still see her and then, thankfully, ran to the opposite side of the road as a space between the vehicles, possibly made by the traffic lights further along the road, appeared. Now to see if she could get the attention of any cars going in the same direction as she was.

A crescent moon was rising now and a few stars were starting to appear, like bits of silver paper stuck on a dark blue background. At least the sky was clear. It might get cold, but that was better than if she had got wet in the earlier rain, she thought. The footpath was easier to walk on and there was a stone wall to her left which provided shelter from the wind. Not a single car stopped, which was disappointing, but the road was beginning to look slightly familiar. Yes! Rita quickened her step. She had just seen a sign. "Welcome to Woodstock" it said. There would be somewhere here where she could get help, she thought, then she had a wedding to get to.

Monday 30th December 2019 4.30 pm

Reaching the tall imposing gates of Blenheim Palace, Rita thought her plan to seek help there might be thwarted. The gates were closed but, thankfully, the pedestrian entrance was still open. She had no phone, so couldn't check the time, but she imagined the grounds closed around sunset. Rita went through the narrow space and started to trudge down the long drive which provided an impressive view of the palace, just as Capability Brown had intended. Over to her right, she knew, was the view of the lake and the bridge that led to the towering monument erected to honour the Duke of Marlborough's victories. When Rita had been here before she had railed against the extravagance and pomp used to celebrate what was essentially the senseless waste of human lives, one country's poor young men fighting another's for the political and commercial advantage of the rich. Still, there was something to be said for class and privilege, she thought. They were bound to have security guards, and they could help her, couldn't they?

No sooner had she thought this, than torchlight shone in her face. She had nearly reached the ticket offices where visitors coughed up the best part of £30 for the privilege of viewing what Sarah Duchess of Marlborough had built with the Government's money to honour her husband.

"The house is closed, Miss." the voice behind the torch said "And the park closes in 15 minutes. Hadn't you better go home?"

"That would be great," said Rita, "But I'm in a bit of trouble you see."

Monday 30th December 2019 5.00pm

The kindly security guard, whose name turned out to be Asif, used his radio to summon up one of the electric buggies the palace staff used to ferry less able customers about the grounds. His friend Jerry, who drove the buggy, was a cheerful soul in khaki shirt and trousers worn with a blue fleece to keep him warm.

"What we got here then, Asif?" he said, "A waif and stray?"

"She's in a bit of bother, Jerry" he replied. "Best get her to the security post and call the police."

"Right you are." said Jerry and, once they were on board, he drove as fast as the cart would allow along the remaining length of the drive, and round the corner to a security hut.

Tuesday 31st December 2019 4.00pm

The day after the siege ended, which was New Year's Eve, the debrief took place at Enderby police station. It was not far short of twenty four hours since Rita Patel had been found. A few of the pieces missing from the investigations into the drugs ring, and into the head found in the cathedral, had fallen into place since then. The meeting took place in a large, windowless, conference room. Seated in rows, theatre style, were numerous officers, some of whom had been involved in the surveillance of the factory. Others were there to be briefed for investigations going forward. None was very pleased at having their new year celebrations disturbed, but crime did not stop for the holidays. Jamie Bridge and Sue Foster were sitting at a table to the side of the dais so they could see the audience and watch the screen on the wall.

With Rita's permission, the presentation included videos of parts of the witness interview she had given earlier that day. Rita had been picked up from Blenheim Palace by Thames Valley Police and, when they had extracted any information she could give about the possible whereabouts of the suspects, which was little, she had been escorted to Leicester. She had arrived back at Elm Drive in the early hours of 31 December wearing a blue forensic suit, having been checked over in a suite in Oxford. All the clothes she was wearing had been bagged in case they yielded any valuable evidence. Her phone was in the possession of Leicestershire police, she was told "You will get it back" Jamie Bridge had assured her when they spoke by video link.

"The outfit suits you, sis!" Nayan had joked when she stumbled out of the police car, her mind still dull after a long nap on the journey.

"Yeh" Mohal joined in," You should definitely wear it to the wedding!"

"Oh Rita!" Padma had no words. She hugged her daughter close, despite the plastic feel of her outfit and the way it creaked when you touched it.

After a few hours' sleep in her own bed, and a welcome shower, Rita had been collected by a patrol car at 9am and questioned all morning, and some of the afternoon, with breaks in between in recognition of the ordeal she had been through. One of the partners at the legal firm had offered to sit in, but she had declined. It would only slow things up. She had finally been released at 3pm. She had climbed into the car provided by the wedding planner and been whisked off to prepare for the ceremony that evening.

"Well done, DC Adams." Jamie Bridge was full of praise for the Detective Constable. "You got Rita's trust and extracted a lot of useful information from her. More than most of the rest of us could have done." He stared around the room, deliberately not catching the eye of the ACC alongside him.

"It is now clear that, as we got closer to their drug processing and distribution network, the perpetrators were prepared to go to extreme lengths to prevent information leaking out to us. The three heads found in different cathedrals – ours, Exeter and Durham - all belonged to informers. Steven Coleman, who was the first to tell us about the use of the disused factory near Abbey Park, had the misfortune to come into contact with DC Yousef Mohamed. He is being processed by Professional Standards "

A photograph of the head found in Leicester Cathedral was followed on the screen by a picture of the now discredited police officer. DCI Bridge had heard he had had lots to say, in the hope of lenient treatment. After his encounter with Superintendent Turner and his team, DCI Bridge thought this was unlikely.

"Mr Coleman was killed mid to late September, because it was around then that parts of his body were found, in a house fire." The Detective Chief Inspector continued. "According to Dr Gabriella Hopkins, the pathologist who examined the head, it must have been kept in a freezer somewhere until it turned up in November. When Coleman gave information to DC Mohamed, he would have alerted Colin Shawcross, the main perpetrator in our patch, to whom Mohamed was passing information about our operations."

The DCI paused to take in a sharp breath and shake his head. It was a shock to have been so undermined by a colleague he had trusted. "Coleman, a drug user probably desperate for money for his next fix, effectively signed his own death warrant. As a criminal lawyer, Shawcross used his access to prisons and police stations to pass on information to the criminal fraternity and to get information in return, staying one step ahead of us, as well as arranging various criminal activities which supported his drug operation. Shawcross arranged for one Leeroy Roberts.."

The DCI paused as Leeroy's photographs at the time of his arrest loomed over the audience from the screen, before continuing, "…to be arrested on an assault charge purely so that he could stab Marty Briggs. Briggs was a prison warder who brought drugs, phones and weapons into the prison at the behest of the drug gang. Ironically, he was stabbed with a weapon he himself had smuggled in."

The screen moved on to a picture of the late prison guard. "He also passed on information to Serious Crimes,"

Jamie Bridge went on, "having done a deal promising him immunity from prosecution, and for that he was killed."

The DCI paused until a picture of a man in his late twenties with a black beard appeared. "James Lomax. Shawcross's brother-in-law," Jamie Bridge introduced him to the audience. "He was also stabbed by Leeroy Roberts, when he was out on bail. Lomax was in logistics, what we used to call haulage. He ran vans and lorries the length and breadth of the country." Jamie Bridge pointed to the image of a large light-brown removal van with 'LOMAX LORRIES' picked out in red on the side. It was such a familiar sight on the motorways that they were hardly noticed, the audience realised.

"Ideal for getting drugs into the UK." the DCI continued. "He seemed to be operating a route through Belgium, but we don't know where the vehicles went after that. The drug squad are looking into it. Since that death, Colin Shawcross took over the running of the distribution network. There seemed to have been a falling out among thieves, and James Lomax came off worse. Some of that falling out may be attributable to Jai Choudhrie, the other man we know who was in the factory." Photographs of Jai and Colin had already appeared in the slide show. "He was getting more senior in the organisation and displacing Lomax, it seems. Shawcross was pretty ruthless in bumping off a member of his family. Thanks to Rita Patel, we can place Jai in Leicester, Durham and Exeter at the time that the heads were left. He wasn't afraid to get his hands dirty, as it were."

"What about the rest of the guy whose head was in our Cathedral?" someone at the back wanted to know.

"Yeh, Inspector Lo has been investigating that aspect." Jamie deferred to an officer in the second row who stood to address the gathering.

"We ID'd the victim as being Steven Coleman, a research scientist and heavy drug user. As you've heard, he was an informer, keeping us aware of some of the dealers in our patch and enabling us to pick up some small fry. The fact he was a grass was discovered when he had the misfortune to meet DC Yousef Mohamed, who was himself working for the drug gang, unfortunately. Professional Standards will be throwing the book at him. We are in touch with the Durham and Devon and Cornwall forces about their heads. It looks like the same story. A grisly warning to others not to inform. Mr Coleman's legs were found in a house fire. We haven't found the rest of him yet. His remains could have been burnt or disposed of in another way. We just don't know." Inspector Lo sat down.

"There was no intelligence on the two main perpetrators, Ma'am? No previous convictions or even warnings?" a bright young DC asked from the third row.

"We were closing in on them, of course, thanks to our informers." Sue Foster smoothed down her uniform jacket with her hands, glad to get an easy question, "But they had never come to police attention, no." she said, then added, "Colin Shawcross was in plain sight, of course, as a criminal lawyer, but gave us no grounds for suspicion. Jai Choudrie only came up in a computer search in relation to a canal barge connected to an abduction a few years ago. We think that was a coincidence."

"Any idea where Shawcross and Choudhrie are now ma'am?" a DI sitting at the front spoke up. ACC Foster squirmed a little in her chair.

"We believe they fled abroad. Since Rita Patel was dropped near Woodstock, we investigated whether they caught a plane from Oxford Airport, which is nearby. It seems possible. Witnesses say there was a lot of activity around a private aircraft on the tarmac that afternoon. We think they left the country and may have ended up in Dubai, perhaps. We just don't know." She spread out the fingers of her upturned hands as if in a gesture of surrender." It was unfortunate that we were short of officers to prevent their escape." So, it was going to be blamed on the cuts, Jamie Bridge thought, not on her incompetence,

"But we disrupted a supply line and we have arrested a few of those we caught on the CCTV as they smuggled equipment out of the disused factory via the river."

Only after you realised there was a traitor in our midst and who it was, Jamie Bridge thought. Sue Foster had no shame in taking credit where none was due.

"And the hostage was unharmed?" another DI in the front row asked Jamie.

"Trissey" he said generously, indicating the young Detective Constable sitting at the end of the second row. "Do you want to take that?"

DC Trissey Adams stood up, "Yes, Rita was none the worse for her ordeal. She was able to get a few hours' sleep before the interview, so she was very coherent. It was a coincidence that Rita Patel knew both Shawcross and Choudhrie, but it may have saved her life. They got away on motorbikes, as you know."

Pictures of BMW bikes similar to those used in the get-away flashed up on the screen as Trissey went on. "The bikes were ridden into the back of a Lomax lorry parked on the nearby housing estate, Rita told us, and the lorry was swapped for a van somewhere en route. Rita was blindfolded by then. It was a well - planned escape." she paused. Before sitting down, DC Adams added," Rita Patel said she was relieved to get out of the factory. I believe she had a wedding to get to."

Chapter

22

"True religion is real living; living with all one's soul, with all one's goodness and righteousness."

Albert Einstein

Wednesday 1ˢᵗ January 2020 12.00 am

"I feel quite emotional!" Rita Patel was smiling, and tears of happiness were trickling down her cheeks, threatening to spoil the elaborate make-up which had been applied late the previous afternoon, once she had been scooped up from the police station, courtesy of Susie Day, the planner, and taken directly to the salon, where her dress and shoes had been waiting all day.

The first of the yellow rockets in the display billed as the 'Wedding and New Year Firework Show' had just been launched. It was swiftly followed by a battery of others, all vying for space in the blackness of the midnight sky. The upturned faces of Rita, her friend Priya, and her brothers, Mohal and Nayan, were lit up in the glow as they stood together watching from the balcony of Belvoir Castle in Leicestershire, where the marriage ceremony had taken place at 5pm. Festivities had ensued since then, and would go on for many hours longer, culminating in a lunch at about 2pm on the day after the wedding. The main participants, and several of the guests, had rooms in the Castle so they could get some rest in between the fireworks and breakfast. If the catering was as good as the celebratory dinner had been that evening, they were in for a treat.

The venue was, in Ayeesha's view 'epic'. 'Wow!' had been all she could say for about 15 minutes after arriving with

Morwenna and Adam. She had excitedly extolled its virtues ever since. The Castle's towers and turrets rose above the Vale of Belvoir like an illustration in a fairy tale. It was absolutely beautiful inside, too. "Once they saw it, nothing else would do." the bride's mother had told Ayeesha. "It is sumptuous" she added with pride.

Ayeesha agreed. She had not realised when she heard about the arrangements that it meant an "actual castle". There had been cannons to the left and right of them and suits of armour at every turn. The ceremony had taken place in one of the state rooms. The ceilings soared, the floors looked like they were made of marble, and the bride and groom seemed to glide over the deep blue velvet carpet on the stairs as they made their way towards the mandap, the canopy under which the ceremony was to take place. Susie Day had tastefully draped the room in gold and yellow fabric and every corner was filled with golden flowers.

"It's bigger than Downton Abbey." Ayeesha hissed to Morwenna during the wedding.

"Yes, I think you mean Highclere Castle in Hampshire." she answered, using her hand to partially cover her mouth as she spoke. "It's definitely bigger than that. They use this castle to stand in for Windsor Castle in the Netflix series The Crown, you know."

"No! Really!" Ayeesha exclaimed and had to be ' Shushed!' by Morwenna as they watched the couple place floral garlands over each other and then exchange rings.

"They could have had cannon fire to end the evening, you know." Nayan said to Ayeesha as they sat opposite one another in one of the state dining rooms for the celebratory dinner which followed the ceremony. "but they opted for fireworks instead. A missed opportunity I would say." The long tables had a river of golden flowers flowing along them and golden fabric was swathed over the heads of the happy pair. Portraits of dukes and duchesses looked down on them. The Duke's sword lay ready for the cutting of the cake. The past and the present had been brought together magnificently, with no expense spared.

His sister knew the history of Belvoir Castle, of course, and had told Nayan all about it at the time the arrangements were made. Belonging to the Duke of Rutland, the same family had lived there for almost a thousand years and still live in part of it, she had told him. The first castle on the site was built in 1067 and given by William the Conqueror to his standard bearer, Robert de Todeni. The manor passed to the Manners family 1508. A new castle was built in 1555 to replace the ruins of the Norman one. The building incorporated stone from Croxton Abbey and Belvoir Priory, which had fallen in the dissolution of the monasteries. King Charles 1 had stayed there during the English Civil War and the castle was destroyed by the Parliamentarians in 1649.

Work on the new building was completed in 1668, after the restoration of the monarchy. A plan to rebuild the castle again in the Romantic Gothic Revival style in 1799 faltered when it was almost destroyed by fire. Many great works of art had been lost in the fire, including paintings by Titian and Rubens. The building was finally competed in 1832. The castle sits in almost 15,000 acres, Rita had said, and the gardens, which had looked beautiful when the family had visited in August to watch the annual pyrotechnic and firework competition, were designed by the 5th Duchess of Rutland in 1799.

It made sense that the fireworks were so good, Nayan was thinking now as he watched them from the balcony with his siblings and their partners. Perhaps the couple had made the right choice in rejecting the cannon he conceded.

"Have you had a good time, Rita?" a gentle voice said from behind her during a lull in the series of explosions. Mahir slipped his hand into hers and lifted it so he could kiss her hennaed fingers, causing the series of bangles on her arm to jangle. The decorative patterns painted all the way along Rita's arm were highlighted in the flare of the next rocket.

"It's been amazing!" she gasped, "I can't believe we're in a new decade!" she went on excitedly, linking a hand with Priya who joined her other hand with Mohal's. Rita's older brother more reluctantly touched the fingertips of his younger brother, Nayan, whose other hand was securely grasped by Jamie Bridge. They looked like a jewelled necklace, Rita thought, in all their bright colours. When the rockets gave way to fountains and streams of fizzing colour, they all unclasped their hands to give their partners a new year kiss. Mahir, looking elegant in his green velvet bandhgalas jacket, with its Nehru collar, bent to kiss his fiancé, Rita, who was looking radiant in her teal-coloured sari. Priya, with a streak of red dye in her hair and wearing a red sari "and a lot of bling", as Morwenna had described it, smiled as she and her new husband, Mohal, dressed in white, enjoyed yet another married embrace. Nayan and his partner, the newly promoted Acting Superintendent Jamie Bridge, in matching blue silk kurta sets, kissed each other with delight.

What would the new year bring for them all? Rita wondered as she nestled against Mahir and stared upwards at the kaleidoscope of colours filling the darkness above them again. The last few months had been eventful. Surely there could not be so many more changes to come? Smoke was drifting down towards them and an acrid smell was filling the air. The smoke made Rita think of the exhaust fumes from the motor bikes in the confined space of the hall in the factory, before they had roared terrifyingly out of the building, Anya sitting behind Colin, and Rita behind Jai. One of the most terrifying moments had been when she had heard the shots of the police as they aimed in vain at the speeding motorbikes. It had all happened barely 36 hours ago. Suddenly Rita gave a shiver.

"Cold?" Mahir asked, concerned. He tried to arrange the

cover around her shoulders to make her warmer. But the thinness of her silk sari was not why she had shivered.

"No" she shook her head, "I was just thinking."

"Oh dear" said Mahir drily, that was not a good thing.

Rita was looking up at the stars and smiling again. Life would always be an adventure, she thought.

ISBN: 978-1-910779-72-9

ISBN: 978-1-910779-73-6

ISBN: 978-1-910779-74-3

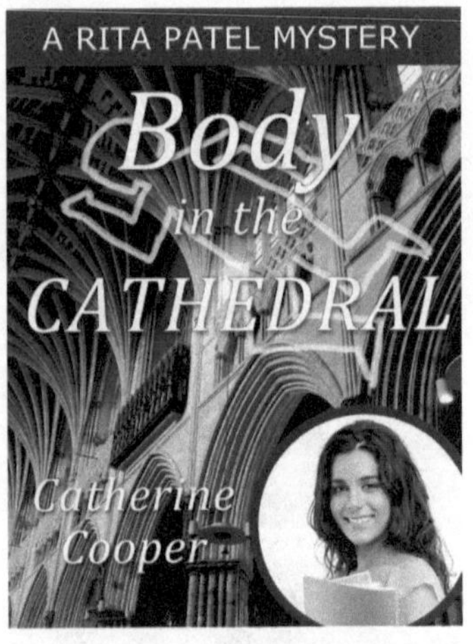

ISBN: 978-1-910779-75-0